A love story you will hate

# Neel *and* Nitin

## NIKHIL KAPOOR

**BLUEROSE PUBLISHERS**
India | U.K.

Copyright © Nikhil Kapoor 2024

All rights reserved by author. No part of this publication may be reproduced, stored in a retrieval system or transmitted in any form or by any means, electronic, mechanical, photocopying, recording or otherwise, without the prior permission of the author. Although every precaution has been taken to verify the accuracy of the information contained herein, the publisher assumes no responsibility for any errors or omissions. No liability is assumed for damages that may result from the use of information contained within.

BlueRose Publishers takes no responsibility for any damages, losses, or liabilities that may arise from the use or misuse of the information, products, or services provided in this publication.

For permissions requests or inquiries regarding this publication, please contact:

BLUEROSE PUBLISHERS
www.BlueRoseONE.com
info@bluerosepublishers.com
+91 8882 898 898
+4407342408967

ISBN: 978-93-6452-211-3

Cover Design: Sadhna Kumari
Typesetting: Pooja Sharma

First Edition: September 2024

# Dedication

To my beloved wife, Meeta Kapoor, whose unwavering support has granted me the freedom to explore the depths of relationships without hesitation. It is through her understanding and trust that I have been able to fully embrace and comprehend the intricate nature of human connections.

# Preface

In a world where love knows no bounds and transcends the constraints of time and circumstance, unfolds the poignant and evocative tale of Nitin and Neel. Their journey is one of deep passion, unspoken truths, and heart-wrenching sacrifices, capturing the very essence of human connection. This narrative weaves through the intricate dance of friendship turned love, exploring the profound impact of unfulfilled desires and the shadows of regret that linger in their wake.

As readers delve into this story, they will find themselves immersed in the emotional highs and lows of Nitin and Nee's lives. From the tender moments of unspoken understanding to the agonizing reality of choices made and paths diverged, every page is imbued with a sense of authenticity and raw emotion. The love shared between these two souls is not just a fleeting romance but a profound bond that challenges societal norms and personal insecurities, ultimately teaching them the true meaning of love and acceptance.

Through the lens of their shared memories and the haunting beauty of their connection, this book invites readers to reflect on their own experiences with love, loss, and the enduring power of the human spirit. It is a testament to the idea that true love, once found, leaves an indelible mark on our hearts, guiding us through life's darkest moments and illuminating our path forward. Prepare to be moved to tears and inspired by the resilience of Nitin and Neil's love, a story that will stay with you long after the final page is turned.

# Prologue

In the heart of a city that never sleeps, where dreams are both born and shattered in the blink of an eye, the night sky stretched over towering buildings like a velvet blanket adorned with twinkling stars. Below, the streets pulsed with life, a ceaseless flow of people chasing ambitions, escaping pasts, or simply trying to survive the moment. It was a world where connections were often fleeting, and the ties that bound people together were easily severed by the passage of time.

But amid this transient existence, there were those rare connections that defied the odds, relationships that endured despite the challenges and changes life inevitably brought. They were forged in the crucible of shared experiences, in the silent understanding of unspoken words, and in the quiet moments where two souls found solace in each other's presence.

This story begins not in the chaos of the city's rush but in the quiet spaces where the echoes of the past linger, where the heart wrestles with memories too powerful to be forgotten. It is a tale of choices made and paths taken, of the invisible threads that connect us to one another in ways we often don't realize until it's too late.

As the sun sets on one chapter, casting long shadows across the lives of those who once stood in its light, the dawn of a new beginning teases the horizon. In the spaces between what was and what could be, this is where the story unfolds, in the delicate balance between holding on and letting go.

# Contents

In the Quiet of Morning ................................................. 1
Shattered trust ............................................................... 4
Broken Bonds .................................................................. 6
Fractured Trust ............................................................... 9
A Beacon in Dark ......................................................... 13
The Rumor Mill's Toll .................................................. 15
The Heart's Confession ............................................... 18
The End of Us ............................................................... 21
Fragments of Friendship ............................................. 25
NEEL ................................................................................ 28
  Beneath The Façade .................................................. 29
  Echoes of Regret ......................................................... 33
  Shadows of Contrition .............................................. 42
NITIN ............................................................................... 44
  A New Path .................................................................. 45
  Whisper Of Absence .................................................. 48

| | |
|---|---|
| A Step Forward | 51 |
| Unspoken Truths | 54 |
| Whispers of Changes | 57 |
| In the Shadow of Rumors | 60 |
| Heart's Heavy Echo | 66 |
| Erased Echoes | 70 |
| Unwavering Support | 73 |
| Dancing Through Life | 77 |
| Eternal Bonds | 80 |
| Fractured Bonds: A Tale of Lost Friendship | 84 |
| **NEEL** | **90** |
| Fractured Souls | 91 |
| Echoes of Friendship | 94 |
| Echoes of Solitude | 103 |
| Behind the Smile | 107 |
| Drifting Tides | 112 |
| **NITIN** | **116** |
| Echoes of the Muse | 117 |
| Fractured Bonds | 120 |
| Fragmented Reflections | 124 |
| Echoes of Longing | 128 |
| Ashes of Echoes | 134 |
| **NEEL** | **137** |
| Eclipsed Flames | 138 |
| Fragments of Fate | 147 |

**NITIN** ............................................................. 150
    Eternal Embrace ............................................ 151
    The Unyielding Bond ................................... 156
    Forever Fades Away ..................................... 159

# In the Quiet of Morning

Nitin stirred, his senses slowly awakening to the gentle caress of dawn filtering through the curtains. As he blinked away the remnants of sleep, he found himself enveloped in a warm embrace, the soft rise and fall of Neel's chest beneath his own.

A faint smile tugged at Nitin's lips as he gazed at Neel's peaceful countenance, the events of the previous night still fresh in his mind. He couldn't shake the memory of their shared intimacy, the tender moments that had unfolded in the quiet of the night.

Memories of the night before flooded back to Nitin's mind, and he winced as he recalled the drunken argument with his now ex-girlfriend. She had stormed off, leaving him alone and angry, until Neel had found him and brought him home.

A wave of guilt washed over Nitin as he realized how he must have burdened Neel with his troubles. But then, in the dim light of dawn, he noticed something else – a tenderness in Neel's touch, a warmth in his gaze that went beyond mere friendship.

With a mixture of awe and trepidation, Nitin shifted closer to Neel, relishing the comforting weight of his presence. Their bodies molded together seamlessly, as if drawn by an invisible force that transcended mere friendship.

Memories of their conversation, their laughter, and the unspoken connection between them danced through Nitin's mind, igniting a spark of something unfamiliar yet undeniably powerful. It was a feeling he couldn't quite articulate, a stirring deep within his soul that left him breathless with longing.

As he lay there, bathed in the soft glow of morning light, Nitin felt a surge of emotion welling up inside him – a potent mixture of desire, fear, and unspoken yearning. He reached out tentatively, his fingers tracing the contours of Neel's face, committing every curve and angle to memory.

Neel stirred beneath his touch, his eyes fluttering open to meet Nitin's gaze. In that moment, time seemed to stand still as they gazed at each other, the air thick with unspoken words and unspoken promises.

Without a word, Nitin leaned in, his lips seeking Neel's in a tender, lingering kiss. It was a testament to everything they had shared, everything they had yet to explore together. And in that stolen moment, amidst the quiet of the morning, Nitin felt the weight of the world lift from his shoulders, replaced by a sense of peace and belonging he had never known before.

As they broke apart, breathless and exhilarated, Nitin knew that this was only the beginning of their journey together. With Neel by his side, he was ready to face whatever the future held, armed with nothing but the certainty of their love.

In the hazy light of dawn, as the world outside stirred to life, Nitin and Neel lay entwined, their hearts beating as one. And as they drifted back to sleep, wrapped in each other's arms, they knew that this – this beautiful, fleeting moment – was where they were meant to be.

# Shattered trust

As Nitin stirred awake in the morning light, his senses slowly coming to life, he found himself wrapped in Neel's embrace. At first, he felt a surge of warmth at the memory of their passionate night together, but as the haze of sleep lifted, reality came crashing down around him like a tidal wave.

With a jolt, Nitin realized what had transpired between them the night before, and a wave of fury coursed through him, hot and unrelenting. How could Neel have taken advantage of him in his intoxicated state? How could he have allowed himself to be so foolish, to let his guard down and succumb to Neel's seduction?

Fueled by anger and betrayal, Nitin exploded into a frenzy of rage, his voice rising to a crescendo as he lashed out at Neel with words that cut deeper than any knife. He accused Neel of manipulating him, of preying on his vulnerabilities for his own selfish desires. He hurled insults and accusations with reckless abandon, each word a dagger aimed straight at Neel's heart.

But as the tirade continued, Nitin's anger began to wane, replaced by a crushing sense of guilt and self-loathing. How could he have allowed himself to be so blind, so naive? How could he have let his feelings cloud his judgment, to the point where he couldn't even recognize the truth staring him in the face?

In the midst of his turmoil, Neel remained silent, his eyes filled with a sadness that cut Nitin to the core. But instead of lashing out in return, Neel simply listened, absorbing Nitin's pain with a quiet strength that spoke volumes. And as Nitin's anger finally spent itself, he was left with nothing but the hollow ache of regret and remorse.

With tears streaming down his face, neel collapsed down , his body wracked with sobs of despair. He begged for forgiveness, for understanding, for a chance to make things right. But deep down, he knew that some wounds ran too deep to ever truly heal, and that no amount of apologies could ever undo the damage he had caused.

# Broken Bonds

Neel's heart plummeted like a stone into the depths of his chest, a mixture of shock and hurt rippling through him as Nitin's words sliced through the air. Each syllable felt like a betrayal, an unraveling of the delicate bond they had shared. How could Nitin reduce their intimate connection to a mere mistake, brushing it off like discarded debris?

Anger surged through Neel in a tempestuous wave, threatening to engulf him in its fiery grip. He recoiled from Nitin, his fists clenching at his sides as he fought to contain the torrent of emotions threatening to consume him. "You can't just dismiss this, Nitin," he growled, his voice low and husky with barely restrained fury. "What we shared was real, it was raw—it was everything."

Each word dripped with accusation, each syllable a barb aimed straight at Nitin's heart. "You can't blame this on the alcohol," Neel continued, his voice rising with each assertion. "You were there, you were present—you wanted it just as much as I did. Don't try to deny it now."

But beneath the veneer of righteous indignation, doubt gnawed at the edges of Neel's resolve. Was it truly just desire driving their actions, or was there something deeper, something more profound at play?

As Nitin's gaze met his, uncertainty flickering in those stormy depths, Neel felt a pang of sadness twist in his chest. Maybe Nitin was right—maybe they were only meant to be friends. But the thought of losing what they had shared, of relinquishing the tender moments they had woven together, tore at Neel's very soul.

With a heavy sigh, Neel turned away, his shoulders slumping with the weight of his emotions. "I'm sorry," he murmured, the words heavy with regret. "I never meant to complicate things, to blur the lines between us."

But as the silence stretched between them, punctuated only by the ragged sounds of their breathing, Neel couldn't help but wonder—where did they go from here? The future stretched out before them like an uncertain path, shrouded in mist and shadow.

Their bond hung in the balance, teetering on the precipice of something unknown. And as Neel grappled with the swirling whirlpool of emotions churning within him, he couldn't shake the feeling that whatever lay ahead would irrevocably alter the course of their lives forever.

The atmosphere crackled with tension as Nitin's accusations hung heavy in the air, each word a dagger aimed straight at Neel's heart. "How could you do this to me, Neel?" Nitin's voice was laced with venom, his eyes blazing with fury. "You took advantage of me, of my vulnerable state. You knew I was intoxicated, and you used that to fulfill your own selfish desires."

Neel recoiled as if struck, his own anger simmering beneath the surface. "That's not true, Nitin," he protested, his voice tinged with desperation. "You wanted this just as much as I did. You were the one who kissed me back, who pulled me closer."

But Nitin wasn't listening, his rage consuming him like a wildfire. With a roar of frustration, he swept his arm across the table, sending objects crashing to the ground in a cacophony of destruction. The picture hanging on the wall caught his eye, a reminder of happier times now tainted by betrayal.

With a primal scream, Nitin lunged forward, tearing the picture from its frame and shredding it into jagged pieces. Each rip echoed like a gunshot in the silent room, a stark testament to the shattered trust between them.

As the last scrap of paper fluttered to the ground, Nitin sank to his knees, his breath ragged and uneven. Tears welled in his eyes, hot and bitter as they spilled down his cheeks. "How could you?" he whispered, his voice raw with anguish. "How could you betray me like this?"

But Neel had no answer, his own heart heavy with guilt and regret. In that moment, as the shattered remnants of their picture lay scattered at their feet, he realized the depth of the chasm that had opened between them. And as he watched Nitin's shoulders shake with silent sobs, he knew that no amount of apologies could ever bridge the divide."

# Fractured Trust

Neel watched in stunned silence as Nitins words pierced through him like arrows, each accusation a dagger to his heart. He could feel the weight of Nitins's disappointment bearing down on him, crushing him beneath its unbearable burden. How had everything unraveled so quickly, so irreparably?

As Nitin turned to leave, his footsteps echoing hollowly in the empty apartment, Neel felt a wave of despair wash over him. His throat tightened, his chest constricted with the agony of loss. This was it – the end of everything they had shared, the end of their friendship, their bond shattered beyond repair.

But as Nitin's parting words echoed in the silence, accusing neel of harboring secret desires beneath the guise of friendship, a spark of defiance flickered to life within him. How dare Nitin suggest such a thing, to twist their shared history into something ugly and deceitful?

With a surge of anger, Neel found his voice, his words cutting through the silence like a blade. "No, Nitin," he declared, his voice trembling with emotion. "You're wrong. I never… I never wanted to hurt you. I never meant for any of this to happen."

But his protests fell on deaf ears as Nitin stormed out, leaving Neel alone in the wake of their shattered friendship. And as the door slammed shut behind him, Neel sank to his knees, his heart breaking into a million jagged pieces.

For what felt like an eternity, Neel remained there, lost in the depths of his despair, his tears staining the floor beneath him. He had betrayed Nitin, betrayed their friendship, and now he was left to face the consequences alone.

But amidst the darkness, a glimmer of hope flickered to life within him – a resolve to make things right, to prove to Nitin that their bond was stronger than any misunderstanding, any accusation. And as he wiped away his tears and gathered the shattered pieces of his heart, Neel knew that he would do whatever it took to win back Nitin's trust, to mend what had been broken, and to rebuild their friendship from the ashes of their shared pain.

Neel stood frozen, his eyes fixed on the retreating figure of Nitinl in the corridor, his heart pounding with a mixture of shock and anguish. "Nitin, wait," he called out, his voice cracking with emotion. "Please, don't go."

But Nitin didn't pause, didn't even glance back as he continued to walk away, his footsteps echoing in the empty apartment like a death knell. "It's over, neel," without looking back he replied, his tone cold and final. "There's nothing left to say."

Desperation clawed at neel's chest, urging him to chase after Nitin, to beg for forgiveness, to explain himself. "No, Nitin, you have to listen to me," he pleaded, his voice thick with tears. "I never meant for any of this to happen. I never wanted to hurt you."

But Nitin's steps never faltered, his resolve unyielding as he reached the door. "Save your excuses, Neel," he spat, his words cutting through the air like a knife. "I trusted you, and you betrayed me. You betrayed our friendship."

With each word, Neel felt the weight of Nitin's accusation bearing down on him, crushing him beneath its unbearable burden. "Nitin, please," he implored, his voice barely a whisper. "I swear, I never... I never had any ulterior motives. I never wanted to hide my feelings from you."

But Nitin had already turned the handle, the door swinging open with a finality that left Nitin reeling. "You always had these feelings, didn't you?" Neel's voice was bitter, accusatory. "You were just using our friendship as a cover."

Nitin's heart clenched at the accusation, his breath catching in his throat as he struggled to find the words to defend himself. "No, Neel, that's not true," he insisted, his voice trembling with emotion. "I care about you, more than anything. I never wanted to lose you."

But Neel was already stepping through the doorway, his form disappearing into the darkness beyond. "I was less

hurt when my girlfriend ditched me than I am right now," he declared, his voice heavy with sorrow. "You've betrayed me, Nitin. And I don't know if I can ever forgive you for that."

And with those final words, Neel was gone, leaving Nitin alone in the silence of the empty apartment, his heart shattered into a million jagged pieces. As tears streamed down his cheeks, he sank to his knees, his hands trembling as he reached out for something – anything – to hold onto.

But there was nothing, nothing but the hollow ache of loss and regret, echoing in the emptiness that surrounded him. And as he buried his face in his hands, Nitin knew that he had lost more than just a friend – he had lost a piece of himself, a piece that he feared he would never be able to reclaim.

# A Beacon in Dark

Neel's hand trembled as it hovered over the sharp blade, his heart weighed down by the unbearable despair crushing his spirit. Tears cascaded down his cheeks, each drop a testament to the agony tearing him apart from within, the echo of his anguish reverberating in the silent confines of the room.

In the suffocating darkness, a voice, soft yet resolute, whispered to him—a voice saturated with love and unwavering hope, urging him to reconsider, to draw strength from the depths of his despair. Love is a beacon in the darkest of nights, it murmured, a beacon that guides you back to the light.

With a shuddering breath, Neel lowered the blade, its menacing gleam fading into obscurity as he crumbled under the weight of his emotions, his sobs wracking his fragile frame. How could he have contemplated extinguishing his own existence, forsaking all chances of redemption and reconciliation?

As memories of happier times flooded his mind—a tapestry woven with laughter, shared dreams, and unspoken promises—Neel's resolve wavered, his heart heavy with regret. How could he even entertain the thought of relinquishing the bond forged over two decades, a bond that had weathered the fiercest of storms?

"It's not worth it," he whispered to himself, his voice a fragile thread in the cacophony of his turmoil. "Love is a flame that must be nurtured, not extinguished. And if my love for Nitin is true, then I must find the courage to fight for it."

With newfound determination igniting his spirit, Neel rose from the depths of his despair, his eyes ablaze with unwavering resolve. "How could I forsake twenty years of shared memories?" he pondered aloud, the words a solemn vow in the solitude of the room.

As he wiped away his tears and steadied his trembling hands, Neel embraced the daunting journey that lay ahead—a journey fraught with uncertainty and pain, yet brimming with the promise of love's enduring strength. For love was not a destination to be reached, but a journey to be embraced, and Neel was prepared to traverse its tumultuous path hand in hand with Nitin, come what may.

# The Rumor Mill's Toll

In one corner of the office, a group of colleagues huddled together, their voices lowered in hushed tones as they exchanged the latest gossip. "I heard they had a falling out," one whispered, her voice tinged with concern as she glanced furtively over her shoulder. "But why?" another chimed in, her eyes wide with curiosity. "They seemed so close!"

"I heard it was about a missed deadline," someone interjected, their tone conspiratorial. "Neel dropped the ball on a major project, and Nitin had to pick up the pieces." The group murmured in agreement, nodding their heads knowingly as they absorbed the juicy tidbit of information.

Meanwhile, in the break room, colleagues exchanged knowing glances over steaming cups of coffee, their hushed conversations punctuated by speculative whispers. "I heard it was a disagreement over creative direction," one ventured, her eyes darting around the room to ensure no one was listening in. "Nitin wanted to take their latest project in one direction, but Neel had other ideas."

"Or maybe it was a clash of egos," another countered, his voice tinged with authority. "They've always been competitive, and maybe this time it went too far." The group leaned in closer, eager to catch every morsel of the tantalizing gossip.

And amidst the chatter of office politics and professional rivalries, a whisper of a different kind began to circulate – a love triangle involving Neel, Nitin, and a mysterious third party. Some speculated that Neel had developed feelings for a coworker, leading to tension between him and Nitin. Others whispered about Nitin's past romantic entanglements resurfacing, causing friction in their once-unbreakable bond.

As the rumors swirled and the gossip mill churned, the atmosphere in the office grew tense, a palpable undercurrent of unease threading its way through the air. Neel and Nitin, once the dynamic duo who had choreographed some of the industry's most iconic songs, now avoided each other like strangers passing in the night.

In every corner of the office, from the water cooler to the copy room, conversations buzzed with speculation about the cause of Neel and Nitin's rift. Some whispered about personal betrayals, while others speculated about professional disagreements. But amidst the myriad theories and conjectures, one thing remained clear – Neel and Nitin's rift had cast a shadow over the office, a shadow that seemed to grow darker with each passing day.

And as the two friends skirted around each other, their once easy camaraderie replaced by awkward silence, the office watched with bated breath, waiting for the inevitable confrontation that would either mend their broken bond or shatter it beyond repair.

# The Heart's Confession

As Neel sat amidst the boxes, his mind weighed down by the turmoil of his decision, his sister Ridhima entered the room, her presence a comforting yet probing presence.

"Neel, what's happening between you and Nitin?" she inquired, her voice laced with concern. "I see the tension, and it's tearing me apart. You two are like brothers to me."

Her words pierced Neel's heart, reminding him of the bond they shared as siblings. He swallowed hard, unable to meet Ridhima's gaze as guilt gnawed at his conscience.

"Ridhima, please," he implored, his voice tinged with desperation. "I don't want to burden you with this. It's complicated, and I need time to sort things out."

But Ridhima refused to back down, her eyes flashing with determination. "Neel, you can't shut me out," she insisted, her voice firm yet gentle. "You and Nitin have been through everything together. Don't let this rift tear you apart. Talk to him, sort things out before it's too late."

Neel's shoulders slumped as he realized he couldn't evade Ridhima's insistence. "Okay, Ridhima," he relented, his tone resigned. "But please, don't involve Nitin. I'll handle this on my own terms."

Ridhima nodded, her expression softening with understanding. "I won't call Nitin," she assured him, her voice soothing. "But promise me, Neel, promise me you'll talk to him before you leave. You owe it to him, and to yourself."

Alone once again, Neel sank onto his bed, the weight of Ridhima's words heavy on his shoulders. How could he explain the turmoil raging within him, the conflicting emotions that threatened to consume him? But as he stared out the window at the city below, a determination blossomed within him.

"I can't do this, Ridhima," Neel protested, his voice trembling with uncertainty. "I don't know if I can face Nitin right now. It's too much."

Ridhima's eyes softened, her hand reaching out to gently squeeze his shoulder. "I understand, Neel," she said softly. "But you can't keep running from this. You need closure, and so does Nitin. Don't let fear dictate your actions."

Torn between his desire to avoid confrontation and his need for resolution, Neel felt the weight of Ridhima's words pressing down on him. Could he muster the courage to face Nitin, to lay bare his heart and confront the pain that had driven them apart?

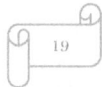

With each passing moment, the inevitability of their meeting loomed larger, casting a shadow over his resolve. But as he contemplated the road ahead, a flicker of determination ignited within him.

"Okay, Ridhima," he said finally, his voice steady with resolve. "I'll talk to Nitin before I leave. But please, give me some time to gather my thoughts."

Ridhima smiled, her eyes shining with pride. "Of course, Neel," she replied, her voice filled with warmth. "Take all the time you need. But remember, I'm here for you, no matter what."

As Ridhima left the room, Neel sank onto his bed, his mind swirling with conflicting emotions. He knew he couldn't avoid confronting Nitin forever, but the thought of facing him filled him with dread. How could he explain the betrayal he felt, the sense of loss that had consumed him?

But as he gazed out the window at the city below, a determination stirred within him. He couldn't let fear dictate his actions. He had to find a way to bridge the chasm that had opened up between them, to salvage what remained of their friendship before it was too late.

With a deep breath, Neel rose to his feet, his resolve firm. He would confront Neel, face the demons that had torn them apart, and find a way to rebuild what had been broken. And as he packed his bags and prepared to leave for London, he knew that no matter what obstacles lay ahead, he would emerge stronger, wiser, and ready to embrace the future, whatever it may hold.

# The End of Us

In the tense atmosphere of the office, colleagues exchanged furtive glances and whispered conversations, their voices hushed with curiosity and apprehension.

"I heard Neel and Nitin had a major falling out," one whispered, her eyes wide with concern as she leaned in closer to her colleague.

"Yeah, something about transferring the company shares," another chimed in, his tone tinged with disbelief. "I never thought they'd let business come between their friendship."

As the rumors swirled, tension hung heavy in the air, casting a pall over the once lively office space. Neel and Nitin's rift had become the talk of the town, their once inseparable bond now shattered into a thousand irreparable pieces.

In the break room, colleagues gathered in small groups, their hushed conversations filled with speculation and gossip.

"I heard Neel offered to transfer his shares to Nitin," one murmured, her brow furrowed in confusion. "But Nitin refused. Can you believe that?"

"It's like watching a soap opera unfold in real life," another remarked, shaking his head in disbelief. "I wonder what went down between them."

But amidst the whispers and conjecture, one thing remained clear – the tension between Neel and Nitin had sent shockwaves through the office, leaving everyone on edge and wondering what would happen next.

Meanwhile, in the midst of the chaos, Neel and Nitin stood face to face, their words dripping with bitterness and regret.

"I don't care what you have to say, Neel," Nitin spat, his voice laced with venom as he turned his back on his former friend. "Our friendship is over, and there's nothing left to salvage."

But Neel refused to back down, his heart heavy with sorrow as he pleaded for a chance to make amends.

"Please, Nitin," he begged, his voice trembling with emotion. "I know I've made mistakes, but I never meant to hurt you. Can't we try to work things out?"

But Nitin's expression remained cold and unyielding, his resolve unshaken by Neel's pleas.

"It's too late for that, Neel," he replied, his voice devoid of emotion as he tore the document in pieces, signifying the end of their partnership. "Our friendship is dead, and there's nothing you can do to change that."

"and please ask Ridhima not to call me again and again , nothing is going to change' nitin almost shouted

"But Ridhima is your sister too, Nitin," Neel cried, desperation creeping into his voice. "She has been tying rakhi to you since we were kids. How can you turn your back on her like this?"

But Nitin's expression remained unmoved, his gaze cold and unyielding as he stared back at Neel. "Our relationship is over, Neel," he declared, his voice steely. "And when it's over, everything associated with it ceases to exist. Including my relationship with Ridhima."

In the midst of their heated exchange, Neel reached into his pocket and withdrew the document, his hands trembling as he held it out to Nitin. "Here," he whispered, his voice barely audible above the tension crackling between them. "I'm transferring my share of the company in your name. It's the least I can do to make things right."

But Nitin's eyes blazed with fury as he snatched the papers from Neel's outstretched hand, tearing them into pieces without a second thought. "I don't need your favors, Neel," he spat, his voice dripping with disdain. "I can make a much bigger company on my own. I don't need you or anyone else to succeed."

Neel's heart clenched at Nitin's words, the sting of betrayal cutting deep. He had hoped that transferring his share of the company would be a gesture of goodwill, a way to mend the rift between them. But now, faced with Nitin's indifference, he realized how futile his efforts had been.

As Neel watched Nitin walk away, his heart shattered into a million pieces, he knew that their friendship was truly lost. And as he sank to his knees, the weight of their broken bond pressing down on him, he couldn't help but wonder if things would ever be the same again.

# Fragments of Friendship

As Neel silently packed his belongings, the weight of their broken friendship bore down on him like a leaden cloak. Each garment he folded, each item he placed aside felt like another piece of their bond slipping away into the abyss of lost memories. The wardrobe, once filled with their intertwined lives, now stood as a stark testament to the chasm that had opened between them.

As he carefully folded Nitin's shirts and placed them in a pile, a wave of nostalgia washed over Neel, engulfing him in a sea of bittersweet remembrance. Each fabric held a story, a shared moment frozen in time – laughter echoing through the room, whispered confessions exchanged in the dead of night, tears shed in moments of vulnerability.

With each item packed away, it felt as though Neel was bidding farewell not just to clothes, but to a lifetime of shared experiences. The weight of their history pressed down on him, a tangible reminder of all they had been and all they had lost.

As he zipped up his suitcase, Neel cast one last lingering glance around the room, his heart heavy with regret and longing. Leaving was the right decision, he knew, but the ache of separation gnawed at his soul. Saying goodbye to Nitin felt like tearing away a piece of himself, leaving behind an irrevocable void.

With a heavy sigh, Neel hoisted his suitcase and made his way to the door, the weight of their broken friendship bearing down on him with every step. It was the end of an era, the end of their once unbreakable bond. But as he crossed the threshold into the unknown, a glimmer of hope flickered in his heart – the hope that someday, somehow, they would find their way back to each other.

Ridhima stood in the doorway, a small wooden box cradled in her hands, her eyes glistening with unshed tears. "Neel, you're forgetting something," she said softly, her voice trembling with emotion. "These are the memories of your friendship with Nitin. Take them with you, or do whatever you need to do with them. But don't leave them behind."

Neel's gaze fell upon the box, its weathered surface bearing the weight of their shared history. With a trembling hand, he reached out to accept it, feeling the weight of their past settling into his palm like a tangible presence. The inscription – "Neel and Nitin's Memories" – blurred before his eyes, a poignant reminder of all they had lost.

As he clutched the box to his chest, Neel felt a flood of emotions wash over him – grief, regret, longing. But beneath it all, there lingered a glimmer of hope – hope that their memories would endure, that their bond would withstand the test of time.

With a heavy heart, Neel turned away, the weight of their memories heavy upon him. But as he stepped into the unknown, he carried with him a flicker of hope – the hope that someday, somehow, they would find their way back to each other, and their memories would once again fill the empty spaces between them.

# NEEL

# Beneath The Façade

As five years elapsed since Neel's arrival in London, his outward demeanor remained unchanged - a beacon of joy and mirth that illuminated every room he entered. To his peers, Neel was akin to a ray of sunshine, radiating warmth and happiness with his infectious laughter and boundless energy. Yet beneath this facade of perpetual cheer, Neel harbored a well of sorrow and despair, concealed from the prying eyes of the world.

During this time, Neel had immersed himself in teaching Indian dance classes, his passion for the art form serving as a temporary respite from the inner turmoil he grappled with. However, despite his outward success and popularity, Neel remained an enigma to those around him, his true emotions shrouded in secrecy.

Ridhima, Neel's ever-observant sister, had relocated to London to pursue her post-graduate studies, her presence serving as a silent source of comfort for her brother. Though she longed to alleviate his pain, she dared not broach the subject that lingered like a dark cloud over their lives. Instead, she offered silent support, hoping that her presence alone would provide solace to Neel in his moments of distress.

But as the years passed and Neel's pain remained unhealed, Ridhima felt compelled to confront the issue that had haunted them both for far too long. Sitting opposite Neel, she gathered her courage and delicately broached the subject that had long been avoided.

"Neel, I understand that it's been difficult for you since what happened with Nitin," Ridhima began gently, her voice infused with sympathy. "But I truly believe that it's time for you to start moving forward with your life."

Neel's brows furrowed in confusion at his sister's words, uncertainty flickering in his eyes. "Moving forward?" he echoed, his voice tinged with apprehension. "What do you mean, Ridhima?"

With a steadying breath, Ridhima forged ahead, her resolve unwavering. "I mean, it's been five years, Neel," she continued, her tone resolute. "You can't keep holding onto the past forever. You need to start seeing someone, start dating again."

Neel's heart clenched at her suggestion, a surge of defiance rising within him. "Dating?" he repeated, his tone laced with bitterness. "You want me to just forget about everything that happened with Nitin and move on as if nothing ever happened?"

Ridhima reached out to touch her brother's hand, her touch gentle yet firm. "Neel, I'm not saying that you should forget about Nitin," she explained softly. "But you can't let what happened between you two hold you back forever. You deserve to be happy, to find someone who loves you for who you are."

Neel's chest tightened with emotion at her words, a torrent of conflicting feelings raging within him. "But what if I don't want to be with anyone else?" he whispered hoarsely, his vulnerability laid bare. "What if Nitin was the only one for me?"

Ridhima's eyes glistened with unshed tears as she met her brother's gaze, her heart aching for his pain. "Neel, I know it's hard," she murmured softly, her voice filled with compassion. "But you can't let fear dictate your life. You have to be willing to take a chance on love again, even if it means risking getting hurt."

A tumult of emotions roiled within Neel as he grappled with his sister's words, his inner turmoil threatening to engulf him. "I can't, Ridhima," he choked out, his voice thick with emotion. "I can't bear the thought of letting someone else in, only to have them leave me like Nitin did."

Tears welled in Ridhima's eyes as she embraced her brother, her heart breaking for his anguish. "I know it's scary, Neel," she whispered, her voice trembling with empathy. "But you're stronger than you think. And I'll be here for you every step of the way, no matter what."

But Neel recoiled from her embrace, his pain and frustration boiling over. "No, Ridhima," he declared sharply, his voice tinged with resentment. "You don't understand. You have no idea what it's like to lose someone you love, to have your heart shattered into a million pieces."

Ridhima's heart constricted at her brother's words, the sting of his rejection piercing her soul. "Neel, please," she implored, her voice trembling with emotion. "I'm just trying to help you. I hate seeing you like this, so lost and broken. I just want you to find some happiness again, that's all."

But Neel shook his head adamantly, his resolve unyielding. "I don't need your pity, Ridhima," he retorted bitterly, his words tinged with defiance. "I don't need anyone's pity. I'll figure things out on my own."

With that final declaration, Neel stormed out of the house, leaving Ridhima alone in the wake of his departure. Tears streamed down her cheeks as she watched him go, her heart heavy with sorrow for the pain her brother carried within him. She knew that Neel had a long and arduous journey ahead of him, one fraught with obstacles and challenges. But she also knew that he possessed the strength and resilience to navigate it, to find his way back to happiness, even if it took him a lifetime.

# Echoes of Regret

The dimly lit bar buzzed with the low hum of conversation and the clinking of glasses as patrons mingled and laughed. Neel sat at the bar, nursing his sixth drink of the night, his thoughts consumed by memories of Nitin. It was the first time he had been to the bar without him, and the absence weighed heavily on his heart.

He couldn't help but remember the days when they would sneak out of the house together, lying to their families and escaping to the bar for a night of drinking. Neel never drank with anyone other than Nitin, knowing that after just two drinks, he would be out like a light. Nitin would often tease him about his low tolerance, but Neel didn't mind. He enjoyed their time together, just the two of them, sharing secrets and dreams over a few drinks.

But tonight was different. Tonight, Neel was alone, drowning his sorrows in alcohol as he tried to forget the pain of their broken friendship. Suddenly, a hand landed on his shoulder, and Neel looked up to see Nitin standing beside him, a drink in his hand.

"Chill, yaar," Nitin said with a grin, giving Neel's shoulder a reassuring squeeze. "If you wanted to drink this much, you should have called me. I know you can't handle it on your own."

Nitin's words washed over Neel like a soothing balm, easing the ache in his heart just a little. He couldn't believe Nitin was here, standing beside him after all this time. His eyes filled with tears as he looked at his friend, his brother, the one person who had always been there for him.

Nitin offered Neel a drink and then leaned in closer, his voice soft and filled with warmth. "I miss you, Neel," he confessed, his eyes shining with emotion. "That's why I came to find you in London. I miss dancing with you, laughing with you, just being with you."

Neel's heart swelled with emotion at Nitin's words, the pain of their past disagreements melting away in the warmth of his friend's love. Without a second thought, Neel leaned in and pressed his lips to Nitin's, the kiss deepening with each passing moment.

Nitin pulled Neel closer, his hands tangling in his hair as he deepened the kiss, pouring all of his love and longing into the embrace. Neel felt a surge of desire course through him, igniting a firestorm of passion that threatened to consume them both.

Their bodies moved together in perfect harmony, their lips and tongues dancing in a sensual rhythm that spoke volumes of their unspoken desires. Neel felt himself losing control, surrendering to the intoxicating rush of pleasure that engulfed them both.

As the kiss broke, Nitin gazed into Neel's eyes, his own filled with a mix of longing and tenderness. "I want you, Neel," he whispered, his voice husky with desire. "I want to be with you, to love you, to make you mine."

Neel's heart pounded in his chest as he heard Nitin's words, his body trembling with anticipation. He had never felt more alive, more wanted, than he did in that moment with Nitin. Without a word, he reached out and took Nitin's hand, silently conveying his own desires.

Together, they left the bar behind, their hands intertwined as they made their way to Nitin's room. The air crackled with electricity between them, each step bringing them closer to the culmination of their desires.

As they entered the room, Nitin pulled Neel into his arms, his touch igniting a firestorm of passion within him. Neel's breath caught in his throat as Nitin pressed his lips to his neck, trailing soft kisses along his jawline and down his throat.

Neel's fingers trembled as he reached out to touch Nitin, tracing the contours of his body with trembling hands. He felt a surge of desire coursing through him, his skin tingling with anticipation as Nitin's hands roamed over him, igniting sparks of pleasure with every touch.

Their bodies moved together in a sensual dance of passion and desire, their kisses growing more urgent and demanding with each passing moment. Neel felt himself losing control, surrendering completely to the intoxicating rush of pleasure that engulfed them both.

As they collapsed onto the bed in a tangled mess of limbs and desire, Neel felt a sense of peace wash over him. In Nitin's arms, he felt whole, complete, as if all the pieces of his shattered heart had finally been put back together.

Nitin held him close, his breath warm against Neel's skin as they lay together in the afterglow of their lovemaking. Neel felt a surge of emotion welling up inside him, tears stinging his eyes as he gazed into Nitin's eyes, his heart overflowing with love.

"I love you, Nitin," he whispered, his voice choked with emotion. "I've always loved you, more than anything in this world."

Nitin's eyes softened with tenderness as he reached out to wipe away Neel's tears, his touch gentle and reassuring. "I love you too, Neel," he murmured, his voice filled with emotion. "And I promise, I'll never leave you again. We'll face whatever comes our way together, as long as we're together."

Their bodies entwined, they lay together in the quiet intimacy of the moment, each lost in their own thoughts and emotions. Neel felt a sense of peace wash over him, a feeling of contentment unlike anything:he had ever experienced before. In Nitin's arms, he found solace, comfort, and a love that transcended all boundaries.

As they lay there together, Neel felt a wave of gratitude wash over him, grateful for this second chance at love, grateful for the opportunity to rebuild their friendship into something even stronger and more profound than before.

Nitin's hand gently caressed Neel's cheek, his touch a silent promise of his unwavering devotion. "I'll always be here for you, Neel," he whispered, his voice filled with sincerity. "No matter what happens, no matter where life takes us, my love for you will never waver."

Neel felt his heart swell with love and gratitude as he gazed into Nitin's eyes, the depth of their connection shining bright in the dim light of the room. In that moment, he knew that they were destined to be together, bound by a love that was as eternal as the stars themselves.

As they lay there in each other's arms, Neel felt a sense of peace settle over him, a feeling of completeness that he had never known before. In Nitin's embrace, he found solace, comfort, and a love that knew no bounds.

Together, they drifted off to sleep, their bodies intertwined as they surrendered to the sweet embrace of slumber. And as Neel closed his eyes, he knew that no matter what challenges lay ahead, they would face them together, hand in hand, hearts entwined forever.

The following morning, Neel awoke to find Nitin still sleeping peacefully beside him, his features relaxed and serene in the soft light of dawn. Gently, Neel brushed a stray lock of hair from Nitin's forehead, his heart swelling with love for the man lying beside him.

As Nitin stirred awake, his eyes fluttering open to meet Neel's gaze, a soft smile graced his lips. "Good morning, my love," he murmured, his voice filled with warmth and affection.

Neel returned his smile, feeling a rush of happiness wash over him at the sight of Nitin's radiant face. "Good morning, my heart," he replied, his voice filled with love.

Their morning was filled with quiet moments of intimacy and tenderness, as they shared breakfast together and talked about their plans for the day. Neel felt a sense of joy and contentment settle over him, knowing that he was exactly where he belonged, with the man he loved more than anything in the world.

As they prepared to leave the room and face the day ahead, Nitin took Neel's hand in his, squeezing it gently as he looked into his eyes. "Thank you, Neel," he said softly, his voice filled with emotion. "Thank you for giving us another chance, for believing in us, for believing in our love."

Neel felt his heart swell with love and gratitude as he looked into Nitin's eyes, knowing that he would do anything to protect their love and keep it alive for all eternity.

Together, hand in hand, they stepped out into the world, ready to face whatever challenges lay ahead with courage, strength, and unwavering love. And as they walked side by side, Neel knew that no matter what trials they may face, they would always have each other, bound together by a love that was as eternal as the stars themselves.

Neel's eyes fluttered open, his head throbbing painfully as he tried to make sense of his surroundings. It wasn't morning yet, and for a moment, he wondered if he was still dreaming. But as he turned over and saw the figure lying next to him, his heart sank.

It wasn't Nitin. It was a stranger, a man he didn't recognize, and panic gripped Neel's heart as he realized what had happened. He must have stumbled back to the room in a drunken haze, mistaking this stranger for Nitin in his intoxicated state.

Neel's stomach churned with nausea as he stumbled out of bed and made his way to the bathroom. Leaning heavily against the sink, he stared into the mirror, his reflection a grim reminder of his own foolishness.

As Neel stood there, his head spinning and his stomach churning, he couldn't shake the image of Nitin's face from his mind. The way he had looked at him with love and longing, the way his touch had ignited a firestorm of passion within him – it all felt like a distant memory now, a dream that had slipped through his fingers like sand.

With a heavy heart, Neel splashed cold water on his face, hoping to wash away the shame and regret that threatened to consume him. But no matter how hard he tried, he couldn't erase the memory of what had happened, the way he had betrayed Nitin and himself in a moment of weakness.

As Neel stared at his reflection in the mirror, his mind raced with thoughts and emotions, each one more painful than the last. How could he have been so foolish, so blind to the consequences of his actions? How could he have let his desire and longing cloud his judgment, leading him down a path of self-destruction?

The sound of a knock at the door jolted Neel out of his reverie, and he quickly composed himself before opening it to find Nitin standing on the other side, his expression a mix of concern and disappointment.

"Nitin," Neel whispered, his voice trembling with emotion. "I… I'm so sorry. I don't know what came over me last night. I never meant to hurt you."

Nitin's eyes bore into Neel's, searching for some sign of sincerity amidst the turmoil of emotions that played across his face. "I trusted you, Neel," he said softly, his voice barely above a whisper. "I trusted you with my heart, with my love, and you… you betrayed that trust."

The weight of Nitin's words hung heavy in the air between them, each syllable a dagger to Neel's already shattered heart. He wanted to reach out, to beg for forgiveness, but he knew that words alone could never mend the damage he had caused.

"I know I messed up, Nitin," Neel said, his voice choked with tears. "I know I don't deserve your forgiveness, but please… please give me another chance. I'll do anything to make things right, to prove to you that I love you."

Nitin's gaze softened slightly at Neel's words, a flicker of hope glimmering in his eyes amidst the pain and betrayal. "I want to believe you, Neel," he admitted, his voice tinged with uncertainty. "But how can I trust you again, knowing that you could so easily throw away everything we had?"

Neel's heart ached at Nitin's words, his own guilt and shame threatening to overwhelm him. "I don't have an answer for that, Nitin," he whispered, his voice barely audible above the pounding of his own heartbeat. "All I can say is that I'm sorry, from the depths of my soul. I'll spend the rest of my life trying to make it up to you, if you'll let me."

For a long moment, there was silence between them, the weight of their shared pain hanging heavy in the air. Then, with a heavy sigh, Nitin stepped forward and enveloped Neel in a tight embrace, his arms a silent promise of forgiveness

"I don't know if I can ever fully trust you again, Neel," Nitin's voice echoed in Neel's mind, his words like a haunting refrain that refused to fade away. "You're a coward, Neel. You always have been, and you always will be. You don't deserve my forgiveness, and you certainly don't deserve my love."

Neel's heart constricted with pain as he stared at his reflection in the mirror, his eyes filled with self-loathing and regret. How could he have let himself fall so far, to become the kind of person who hurt the ones he loved most?

As the hallucination of Nitin continued to taunt and ridicule him, Neel felt a surge of anger and frustration welling up inside him. "Stop it," he muttered through gritted teeth, his hands trembling with emotion. "Just… just leave me alone."

But the vision of Nitin only sneered at him, his mocking laughter ringing in Neel's ears as he turned away in defeat, the weight of his own mistakes crushing him like a ton of bricks.

# Shadows of Contrition

In the flickering lights of the future, Neel found solace in the pulsating rhythm of his exuberant dance. His movements were fluid, his steps guided by the intoxicating beat of the music. Each twist and turn was a fervent attempt to drown out the memories of the previous night, to lose himself in the euphoria of the present moment.

As he twirled and leaped across the dance floor, Neel felt a sense of liberation wash over him. The weight of his past mistakes seemed to lift from his shoulders, replaced by a newfound sense of freedom. For a brief moment, he was able to forget the pain and heartache that had plagued him for so long.

But deep down, beneath the facade of carefree abandon, Neel was haunted by the memory of his actions. The events of the previous night loomed large in his mind, casting a shadow over his euphoria. Try as he might, he could not shake the feeling of guilt that gnawed at his conscience.

It was a scene filled with raw emotion, a poignant reminder of the bond that had once united them. Neel stood frozen, his heart torn between conflicting emotions. On one hand, he longed to embrace Nitin, to seek solace in his arms and beg for forgiveness. On the other hand, he felt a surge of defiance, a stubborn refusal to relinquish his independence and admit his mistakes.

As the music faded and the lights dimmed, Neel was left standing alone in the darkness, his mind awash with uncertainty. The dance of forgotten memories had brought him no closer to resolution, no closer to absolution. And as he retreated into the shadows, he knew that the echoes of the past would continue to haunt him, long after the music had stopped.

NITIN

# A New Path

In the bustling corridors of NN Academy, Nitin's footsteps echoed with the weight of his decision, each step a deliberate affirmation of the path he had chosen. As he passed by the reception area, his gaze lingered on the newly installed signage proudly proclaiming the academy's updated name. The removal of one 'N' seemed insignificant to the casual observer, but for Nitin, it marked a profound shift, a symbolic gesture of both liberation and remorse.

The sound of whispers followed him like a haunting refrain, a chorus of speculation and uncertainty swirling around him. Employees exchanged furtive glances, their hushed conversations filled with curiosity and apprehension. Some dared to question the reason behind the alteration, while others simply observed in silent contemplation, wary of the changes unfolding before them.

But amidst the chaos of the office, Nitin's mind was consumed by a tumult of conflicting emotions. The decision to change the name was not merely a matter of branding or corporate identity—it was a reflection of his inner turmoil, a battle between love and hate, loyalty and betrayal.

As he entered his office, Nitin found himself surrounded by the remnants of the past, the stationery bearing the now obsolete 'NN' logo serving as a stark reminder of his tangled emotions. With trembling hands, he began the arduous task of replacing each item, each pen and letterhead, with the new 'N' emblem.

With each stroke of the pen and each click of the mouse, Nitin grappled with the memories that threatened to overwhelm him. The love he once felt for Neel mingled with the resentment and anger that had festered in his heart, creating a maelstrom of conflicting desires.

But as the last 'N' was replaced with the solitary letter 'N', Nitin felt a sense of closure wash over him. It was a small gesture, perhaps, but it was a step towards acceptance, towards embracing the future without being shackled by the past.

And as he stood amidst the newly branded surroundings of NN Academy, Nitin knew that the journey ahead would be fraught with challenges and uncertainties. But he also knew that he was ready to face them head-on, armed with the strength born of love, loss, and ultimately, redemption.

In the press room, journalists were abuzz with anticipation, their pens poised over notepads as they eagerly discussed the latest upheaval at NN Academy. The air crackled with energy as headlines were drafted, each vying to capture the seismic shift unfolding within the company. Nitin's decision had ignited a firestorm of curiosity and intrigue, leaving reporters hungry to unearth the truth behind the enigmatic change.

Meanwhile, in his office, Nitin sat surrounded by the familiar trappings of his professional domain, but the atmosphere was charged with an undercurrent of tension. Despite his outward facade of confidence, he couldn't shake the gnawing sense of unease that gripped him like a vice. Every notification that flashed across his phone screen served as a stark reminder of the relentless scrutiny and speculation swirling around him.

Yet, amidst the relentless onslaught of attention and doubt, Nitin remained steadfast in his resolve. With every fiber of his being, he clung to his decision, steeling himself against the storm of uncertainty that threatened to engulf him. For in the heart of chaos, he found a glimmer of purpose, a steadfast determination to chart a new course, no matter the obstacles that lay ahead.

# Whisper Of Absence

Outside the towering walls of NN Academy, the city pulsed with the rhythm of chatter and speculation. From bustling coffee shops to hushed boardrooms, everyone had an opinion on Nitin's audacious rebranding. Some hailed his boldness and hailed it as a stroke of genius, while others cynically questioned the motives lurking beneath the surface.

But amidst the cacophony of voices, Nitin stood unwavering in his conviction, a solitary figure amidst the storm of public opinion. For him, the decision to shed one 'N' was more than a mere act of rebranding – it was a testament to his unwavering commitment to shaping the destiny of NN Academy, despite the chorus of skepticism that surrounded him.

As the day unfolded, Nitin found himself immersed in a sea of reflections, each wave carrying him deeper into the tumultuous waters of his own thoughts. The journey that had led to this pivotal moment had been fraught with obstacles and challenges, yet with every setback,

Nitin had emerged stronger, more resolute in his purpose.

In the hushed confines of his office, Nitin allowed himself a fleeting moment of introspection, a rare glimpse into the depths of his own soul. Despite the facade of unwavering confidence he projected to the world, he couldn't shake the lingering sense of emptiness that gnawed at his spirit.

Beneath the veneer of success and achievement, Nitin grappled with the haunting specter of loneliness, the absence of Neel casting a long shadow over his every endeavor. With each passing day, the void left by his former friend seemed to widen, a silent reminder of the bond they had once shared.

Yet, even as doubt and insecurity threatened to consume him, Nitin refused to waver from his path.

As Nitin delved deeper into the heart of the bustling city, the cacophony of noise faded into the background, replaced by a deafening silence that echoed the turmoil within him. Each step felt heavier than the last, burdened by the weight of his decision and the uncertainty that lay ahead.

In the quiet solitude of his office, Nitin allowed himself a moment of introspection, a chance to acknowledge the significance of his decision. Despite the uncertainty that lay ahead, he was confident in his ability to lead NN Academy into a new era of growth and success.

But deep down, beneath the facade of confidence and determination, Nitin couldn't shake the nagging sense of emptiness that gnawed at his soul. With each passing day, the void left by Neel's absence seemed to grow larger, a constant reminder of the bond they had once shared.

Despite his outward appearance of strength, Nitin was plagued by doubts and insecurities, his heart heavy with the weight of loneliness. But as he stared out the window, lost in thought, he knew that he could never fully fill the void left by Neel's absence.

# A Step Forward

Outside the towering walls of NN Academy, the city pulsed with the rhythm of chatter and speculation. From bustling coffee shops to hushed boardrooms, everyone had an opinion on Nitin's audacious rebranding. Some hailed his boldness and hailed it as a stroke of genius, while others cynically questioned the motives lurking beneath the surface.

But amidst the cacophony of voices, Nitin stood unwavering in his conviction, a solitary figure amidst the storm of public opinion. For him, the decision to shed one 'N' was more than a mere act of rebranding – it was a testament to his unwavering commitment to shaping the destiny of NN Academy, despite the chorus of skepticism that surrounded him.

As the day unfolded, Nitin found himself immersed in a sea of reflections, each wave carrying him deeper into the tumultuous waters of his own thoughts. The journey that had led to this pivotal moment had been fraught with obstacles and challenges, yet with every setback,

Nitin had emerged stronger, more resolute in his purpose.

In the hushed confines of his office, Nitin allowed himself a fleeting moment of introspection, a rare glimpse into the depths of his own soul. Despite the facade of unwavering confidence he projected to the world, he couldn't shake the lingering sense of emptiness that gnawed at his spirit.

Beneath the veneer of success and achievement, Nitin grappled with the haunting specter of loneliness, the absence of Neel casting a long shadow over his every endeavor. With each passing day, the void left by his former friend seemed to widen, a silent reminder of the bond they had once shared.

Yet, even as doubt and insecurity threatened to consume him, Nitin refused to waver from his path.

As Nitin delved deeper into the heart of the bustling city, the cacophony of noise faded into the background, replaced by a deafening silence that echoed the turmoil within him. Each step felt heavier than the last, burdened by the weight of his decision and the uncertainty that lay ahead.

In the quiet solitude of his office, Nitin allowed himself a moment of introspection, a chance to acknowledge the significance of his decision. Despite the uncertainty that lay ahead, he was confident in his ability to lead NN Academy into a new era of growth and success.

But deep down, beneath the facade of confidence and determination, Nitin couldn't shake the nagging sense of emptiness that gnawed at his soul. With each passing day, the void left by Neel's absence seemed to grow larger, a constant reminder of the bond they had once shared.

Despite his outward appearance of strength, Nitin was plagued by doubts and insecurities, his heart heavy with the weight of loneliness. But as he stared out the window, lost in thought, he knew that he could never fully fill the void left by Neel's absence.

# Unspoken Truths

Nitin sat at the kitchen table, his mother bustling around him as she prepared dinner. The tension in the air was palpable, a silent barrier separating them from the unspoken truth that hung between them like a heavy fog.

"Mom," Nitin began tentatively, breaking the uneasy silence that had settled over them. "I know you've been worried about me, about everything that's been happening."

His mother turned to him, her expression a mixture of concern and affection. "Of course, beta," she replied softly, her eyes searching his face for signs of the turmoil that raged within him. "I just want what's best for you. I want you to be happy."

Nitin swallowed hard, the weight of his mother's words pressing down on him like a leaden weight. "I know, Mom," he murmured, his voice barely above a whisper. "But I don't know if I can go back. I don't know if things can ever be the same."

His mother placed a comforting hand on his shoulder, her touch a soothing balm to his troubled soul. "Sometimes, beta, the hardest decisions are the ones we need to make for ourselves," she said gently. "But that doesn't mean they're easy. It doesn't mean we don't second-guess ourselves, or wonder if we've made the right choice."

Nitin felt a lump form in his throat, the tears threatening to spill over as he struggled to contain the flood of emotions that threatened to overwhelm him. "But what if I've made a mistake, Mom?" he whispered, his voice choked with uncertainty. "What if I've let my pride get in the way of what's truly important?"

His mother's eyes softened with understanding, her gaze unwavering as she met his gaze with unwavering love and support. "Beta, no decision is ever set in stone," she replied, her voice steady and reassuring. "If you feel like you've made a mistake, if you feel like there's still a chance to make things right, then don't be afraid to take it."

Nitin shook his head, unable to accept his mother's words. "But I'm not wrong, Mom," he insisted, his voice tinged with stubbornness. "Neel is the one who's changed, who's turned his back on everything we shared. I can't go back to that, to pretending like nothing ever happened."

His mother sighed, her heart heavy with sorrow as she watched her son struggle with his inner demons. "Beta, I know it's hard to see things clearly right now," she said gently. "But sometimes, the hardest thing to do is to admit when we're wrong, to let go of our pride and ego, and to reach out for forgiveness."

Nitin's jaw clenched, his fists balling at his sides as he fought against the tide of emotions that threatened to consume him. "I can't, Mom," he whispered, his voice barely audible above the pounding of his own heartbeat. "I can't go back to him, not after everything that's happened."

His mother's heart broke for him, her eyes shimmering with unshed tears as she wrapped him in a tight embrace. "I love you, beta," she murmured, her voice choked with emotion. "And no matter what happens, no matter where life takes you, remember that I'll always be here for you, to support you, to guide you, and to love you unconditionally."

# Whispers of Changes

In the pulsating heart of the film industry, Nitin's presence commanded attention, his every step echoing with the anticipation of imminent change. As he navigated the bustling corridors of N Academy, whispers trailed in his wake, a chorus of speculation and intrigue that seemed to follow him like a shadow.

His mother, a silent observer from afar, watched with a mix of pride and apprehension. "Nitin, beta," she murmured softly, her voice a gentle reminder of her maternal concern, "are you certain about this path you're taking?"

Nitin paused, his expression guarded as he met his mother's gaze. "Ma, trust me," he reassured her, his voice unwavering in its conviction. "This is a necessary step forward."

But beneath his confident facade, a flicker of doubt danced in Nitin's eyes, a silent acknowledgment of the uncertainty that lurked within. His mother's words lingered like a haunting refrain, a reminder of the fragility of friendship and the importance of staying true to oneself.

Meanwhile, within the inner sanctum of the film world, whispers of Nitin's exploits swirled like wildfire, each tale more scandalous than the last. Actresses traded stories of fleeting encounters and empty promises, painting Nitin as a master of seduction and manipulation.

"He's a player, plain and simple," one actress declared, her tone tinged with bitterness. "No heart, no soul, just a hollow shell of a man."

Her companion nodded in solemn agreement, her own experiences with Nitin leaving a bitter taste in her mouth. "I fell for his charm once," she admitted, her voice heavy with regret. "But behind his smooth exterior lies a void that no amount of fame or fortune can fill."

Their words reverberated through the hallowed halls of the academy, a sobering reminder of the darker side of Nitin's persona. But Nitin remained oblivious to the gossip that swirled around him, his focus unwavering as he pursued his ambitions with single-minded determination.

Yet deep within him, a seed of doubt had been planted, a nagging suspicion that threatened to unravel the carefully crafted facade he presented to the world. As he gazed out at the glittering skyline beyond, he couldn't shake the feeling that he was on the precipice of a profound reckoning, one that would force him to confront the truth of who he truly was.

And so, amidst the whirlwind of fame and ambition, Nitin found himself standing at a crossroads, torn between the allure of success and the call of his own conscience. The whispers of change grew louder with each passing moment, a relentless reminder that in the world of glamour and illusion, nothing was ever as it seemed.

# In the Shadow of Rumors

Nitin sat in his opulent living room, surrounded by the trappings of his success, yet the weight of his mother's words hung heavy in the air. She stood before him, her expression a mix of concern and disappointment as she addressed the elephant in the room.

"Nitin, beta," she began, her voice gentle but firm, "I know you think you're untouchable, but your reputation is at stake here. You can't afford to ignore the rumors and gossip that are swirling around you."

Nitin's brow furrowed in frustration, his defenses rising instinctively. "Ma, you know how the media works," he protested, his tone defensive. "They'll twist anything to sell a story. I can't be held responsible for their lies and exaggerations."

His mother sighed, her eyes filled with a mother's wisdom born of years of experience. "I understand, beta, but perception is everything in this industry," she replied, her voice tinged with urgency. "If you don't address these rumors head-on, they'll only continue to fester and grow."

Nitin shifted uncomfortably in his seat, the weight of his mother's words pressing down on him like a leaden cloak. "What do you suggest I do, Ma?" he asked, his tone resigned. "Hold a press conference and deny everything? It'll only give them more ammunition."

His mother shook her head, her gaze unwavering as she met his eyes. "No, beta, not a denial, but a clarification," she explained, her voice steady. "You need to set the record straight, once and for all. Address the rumors, dispel the doubts, and put an end to the speculation."

Nitin bristled at the suggestion, his pride wounded by the thought of having to bow to public scrutiny. "But Ma, why should I have to explain myself to anyone?" he protested, his frustration boiling over. "I've worked hard to get where I am, and I won't let anyone tarnish my reputation."

His mother placed a hand on his shoulder, her touch a comforting anchor in the storm of his emotions. "Beta, sometimes we have to do things we don't want to do in order to protect what's important to us," she said softly, her words carrying the weight of maternal wisdom. "And right now, your reputation is at stake."

Nitin sighed, his resolve faltering in the face of his mother's unwavering conviction. "Okay, Ma," he conceded, his voice heavy with resignation. "I'll do it, but just this once. After that, I don't want to hear another word about it."

His mother smiled, her eyes shining with pride and relief. "Thank you, beta," she said, her voice filled with gratitude. "I know it's not easy, but trust me, it's the right thing to do."

And as they sat together in the quiet of the evening, mother and son, united in their determination to protect what mattered most, Nitin couldn't help but feel a glimmer of hope amidst the storm of uncertainty that surrounded him. For in his mother's unwavering support, he found the strength to face whatever challenges lay ahead, knowing that he didn't have to weather the storm alone.

# A Step Forward

In the grand ballroom of a prestigious hotel, the stage was set for Nitin's press conference, a highly anticipated event that promised to shed light on the recent changes at NN Academy. Reporters from various media outlets crowded the room, their cameras poised and notepads ready, eager to capture every word and expression.

As Nitin stepped onto the stage, the room erupted into a flurry of activity. Flashbulbs illuminated the space, casting an ethereal glow around him as he took his place behind the podium. His demeanor was composed, his expression unreadable, as he prepared to face the barrage of questions that awaited him.

The first reporter raised her hand, her voice cutting through the silence like a knife. "Mr. Nitin, can you please explain the rationale behind the decision to remove one 'N' from NN Academy's name?"

Nitin's gaze swept across the room, his eyes meeting each reporter's in turn. "The decision to rebrand NN Academy was a strategic one, aimed at modernizing our image and aligning with our vision for the future," he replied, his voice steady and unwavering.

But amidst the professional inquiries, there were whispers of a more personal nature, questions that probed into Nitin's private life and relationships. One reporter dared to ask, "Mr. Nitin, rumors have been circulating about your friendship with Neel. Can you comment on the nature of your relationship?"

Nitin's facade remained unchanged, his features carefully schooled into neutrality. "My personal relationships are just that – personal," he replied, his tone firm but polite. "I prefer to keep them separate from my professional endeavors."

But the reporters were relentless, their questions growing more intrusive with each passing moment. "Mr. Nitin, there have been reports of tension between you and Neel leading up to his departure from NN Academy. Can you shed some light on what happened?"

Nitin felt a twinge of discomfort at the mention of Neel's name, his heart clenching with regret. "Neel's departure was a mutual decision reached after careful consideration," he replied, choosing his words with care. "We remain on amicable terms, and I wish him all the best in his future endeavors."

But as the questions continued to pour in, Nitin's composure began to falter. "Mr. Nitin, are you denying the allegations of a romantic relationship with Neel?" one reporter pressed, her voice tinged with skepticism.

Nitin's jaw clenched at the insinuation, his patience wearing thin. "I will not dignify such baseless rumors with a response," he retorted, his tone sharp and cutting. "My focus is on leading NN Academy into a bright and prosperous future, and I will not allow gossip to distract from that mission."

As the press conference drew to a close, Nitin felt a sense of relief wash over him. The barrage of questions had taken its toll, but he had weathered the storm with dignity and grace. As he stepped down from the stage, he knew that the challenges ahead would be daunting, but he was determined to face them head-on, guided by his unwavering commitment to NN Academy's success.

# Heart's Heavy Echo

Nitin stumbled into his drawing room, his senses dulled by the intoxicating haze that clouded his mind. His voice echoed off the walls as he screamed, his words laced with bitterness and despair.

"Neel, I know the recording of today's press conference must have reached you by now. This was my final answer to you. It's better for you to start living your life without any expectations."

His mother hurried into the room, her heart heavy with concern as she rushed to comfort him. "If Neel has left your life, then why do you keep a second glass always in front of you?" she implored.

She gently reached out to steady him, her touch a soothing balm against the storm raging within him. "Why do you sleep wearing Neel's T-shirt every night? How long will you continue deceiving yourself like this? Your love is evident even in your anger."

Her words pierced through the haze of his drunken stupor, forcing Nitin to confront the painful truth that lay buried deep within his heart. With a heavy sigh, he smashed the second glass against the floor, shattering it into a thousand irreparable pieces.

"Look, I've ended this wait too," he declared bitterly, his voice raw with emotion. "Now, there's no need for Neel even in my intoxication."

As Nitin stood amidst the shattered fragments of glass, his heart weighed down by a mixture of sorrow and anger, he felt an unyielding resolve hardening within him. His mother's words, though filled with love and concern, seemed to fall on deaf ears, unable to penetrate the wall of hurt and betrayal that surrounded him.

Tears flowed freely down Nitin's cheeks, each drop a testament to the pain he carried within him. He couldn't bring himself to accept his mother's plea, his mind stubbornly clinging to the belief that he had been wronged. The shattered glass beneath his feet mirrored the brokenness he felt inside, a tangible reminder of the shattered trust that had once bound him to Neel.

With a heavy heart and a soul weighed down by grief, Nitin braced himself for the long road ahead. This was not a new beginning, but rather a continuation of the anguish and heartache that had consumed him since the moment he felt Neel's betrayal. And as he took those first tentative steps forward, he did so with a steely determination, unwilling to let go of the pain that had become his constant companion.

"Nitin, both your name begin and end with 'N'. You're forgetting that your first and last friendship is with Neel," his mother said, sitting across from him.

"No, my first and last mistake— and the difference here is that I'll have to live with this mistake for a lifetime," Nitin replied, refilling his glass.

As the room fell into a heavy silence, Nitin's mother sighed, her heart breaking for her son. She knew that he was trapped in a cycle of pain and resentment, unable to break free from the grip of his past. But she also knew that she couldn't force him to confront his feelings – he would have to find his own path to healing.

"Nitin, my son," she said softly, reaching out to touch his hand, "I know that you're hurting. But you can't keep holding onto this anger and bitterness. It's only hurting you in the end."

Nitin shook his head, his eyes clouded with tears. "I can't let go, Ma," he whispered, his voice choked with emotion. "I can't forgive him for what he did to me."

His mother's heart ached at the pain in his voice, wishing she could take away his suffering. "I understand, beta," she replied, her voice gentle yet firm. "But holding onto this anger is only poisoning your own heart. You deserve to be free from this burden."

Nitin looked into his mother's eyes, seeing the love and concern reflected in her gaze. In that moment, he felt a flicker of hope ignite within him – a glimmer of possibility that maybe, just maybe, he could find a way to move forward.

"I'll try, Ma," he said softly, his voice filled with determination. "I'll try to let go of the past and start anew."

His mother smiled, a tear slipping down her cheek. "That's all I ask, beta," she whispered, squeezing his hand gently. "I'll be here for you every step of the way, no matter what."

And as they sat together in the quiet of the room, mother and son, they both knew that healing would take time. But with love and support guiding them, they were ready to face whatever challenges lay ahead, knowing that they would emerge stronger together.

# Erased Echoes

Nitin, I'm your friend. Whether anyone in the class befriends you or not, I'll always be by your side," Neel said, holding Nitin's hand.

It was Nitin's first day at this school. He didn't want to leave his old school, but due to his father's transfer, they had to shift.

"Aunty, you go. I'll take care of Nitin," Neel said, wrapping his arms around Nitin.

Neel stood his ground, a protective barrier between Nitin and the two looming figures of Rohan and Prashant. The air crackled with tension as he faced down the notorious bullies of the school.

"Leave him alone! Nitin is my friend, and I won't stand by while you bully him," Neel's voice rang out, firm and unwavering.

Rohan, the ringleader of the bullies, sneered. "What are you going to do about it, Neel? You're outnumbered!"

Undeterred, Neel met Rohan's gaze with steely resolve. "I don't care. Nitin, come with me. We don't need to deal with these bullies."

A smirk played on Prashant's lips as he stepped forward, flanking Rohan. "Look at this little hero, standing up for his friend. How cute."

Though outnumbered and facing hostility, Neel stood tall, his stance unwavering. "Cute or not, I won't let you pick on someone weaker than you."

Nitin watched, torn between gratitude for Neel's defense and fear of further retaliation from the bullies. Rohan's eyes narrowed, a dangerous glint flashing in them.

"You think you're tough, Neel? Let's see how tough you are when you're all alone," Rohan taunted, taking a menacing step closer.

Neel's fists clenched at his sides, but his resolve remained unshaken. "I won't back down. And Nitin won't be alone. I'm here for him."

With a final glare at the bullies, Neel took Nitin by the arm and led him away from the confrontation, leaving Rohan and Prashant seething with frustration.

"Thanks, Neel. I didn't know what to do," Nitin said, his voice tinged with gratitude and relief.

Neel offered a reassuring smile. "Don't worry, Nitin. I've got your back. Always."

As Nitin sat alone in his dimly lit room, memories of his first meeting with Neel flooded his mind like a torrential downpour. He could still vividly recall the moment they had become friends in school, bonding over shared

interests and dreams of the future. But as he scrolled through the countless photos stored on his phone, each image capturing moments of laughter and camaraderie with Neel, a sense of overwhelming sadness washed over him. With a heavy heart, Nitin began the painful task of deleting each and every picture of their time together, erasing the tangible reminders of a friendship that had once meant everything to him. Each swipe felt like a dagger to his soul, a painful acknowledgment of the irreparable rift that had formed between them. And as the last image vanished from his screen, Nitin felt a profound sense of loss settle over him, the weight of their broken bond bearing down on his shoulders like a crushing burden.

............

# Unwavering Support

Nitin fidgeted nervously, his hands trembling as he stared at the crowded room, his anxiety palpable. Neel stood by his side, offering a steady presence amidst the sea of faces.

"I can't do this presentation, Neel. What if everyone laughs at me?" Nitin whispered, his voice laced with doubt and fear.

Neel placed a reassuring hand on Nitin's shoulder, his expression encouraging. "You got this, Nitin. Just take a deep breath and imagine you're talking only to me. I believe in you."

Nitin's eyes flickered with uncertainty, but he nodded slowly, his confidence bolstered by Neel's unwavering support. "Thanks, Neel. I'll give it my best shot."

As the presentation began, Nitin took a deep breath, steeling himself against the nerves that threatened to overwhelm him. With Neel's words echoing in his mind, he started to speak, his voice gaining strength with each passing moment.

As Nitin delved into the content of his presentation, his nerves began to dissipate, replaced by a growing sense of confidence. The audience listened intently, their attention captured by Nitin's passionate delivery and well-researched material.

Neel watched proudly from the sidelines, his belief in Nitin never wavering. With each word spoken, Nitin grew more assured, his initial doubts fading into the background as he found his rhythm.

As the presentation drew to a close, Nitin glanced at Neel, a grateful smile playing on his lips. "Thanks for believing in me, Neel. I couldn't have done it without you."

Neel returned the smile, his pride evident in his eyes. "You did great, Nitin. I knew you had it in you all along."

With Neel's support and encouragement, Nitin had overcome his fears and delivered a presentation that left a lasting impression on everyone in the room. As they left the auditorium together, Nitin walked a little taller, his confidence buoyed by the knowledge that he had a friend like Neel by his side.

In the dimly lit room, Nitin sat surrounded by shelves filled with trophies and certificates from his school days, each one a testament to his past achievements. His mother, sitting across from him, watched with a heavy heart as he sifted through the memories of his youth.

"Mom, please ask Kailash to throw all these school certificates and medals," Nitin said, his voice tinged with resignation. "I don't need them anymore. They're just taking up space in my cupboard."

His mother's eyes welled with tears as she listened to his words, the weight of his sorrow palpable in the air. "But beta, these are reminders of all the hard work you put in," she protested gently, her voice quivering with emotion. "You earned each and every one of these achievements."

Nitin shook his head, a bitter smile playing at the corners of his lips. "What good are these certificates and medals now, Mom?" he asked, his voice heavy with regret. "They can't bring back what I've lost. They can't mend the broken pieces of my heart."

His mother reached out to touch his hand, her touch a soothing balm against the ache of his grief. "I understand, beta," she murmured, her voice filled with sympathy. "But don't you see? These certificates and medals are a part of who you are. They're a reminder of the person you were before all of this."

Nitin's eyes clouded with tears as he looked at his mother, the weight of his pain written plainly on his face. "I don't want to be that person anymore, Mom," he confessed, his voice barely above a whisper. "I want to move forward, to leave the past behind me."

His mother squeezed his hand gently, her heart breaking for the son she loved so dearly. "I understand, beta," she said softly. "I'll ask Kailash to take care of them for you. But remember, no matter what happens, you will always be my son, and I will always be proud of you."

With a heavy sigh, Nitin nodded, a sense of peace washing over him as he let go of the relics of his past. In that moment, he knew that he was ready to embrace the future, whatever it may hold. And as he looked into his mother's eyes, he found solace in the love and understanding she offered him, a beacon of hope in the darkness of his grief.

# Dancing Through Life

Neel and Nitin stood side by side, their hearts drumming a rhythm of anticipation as they lingered in the backstage shadows, waiting for their moment to shine at the school's talent show.

Nitin's gaze flitted to Neel, a flicker of nervousness dancing in his eyes. "What if we falter, Neel? What if we stumble in front of everyone?"

Neel's hand found Nitin's, a gentle anchor amidst the whirlwind of nerves. "Trust me, Nitin. We've rehearsed tirelessly, pouring our souls into every step. We'll dance like we've never danced before."

The soft melody of a piano filled the air, and Neel and Nitin stepped onto the stage, bathed in the warm glow of the spotlight. Their movements were a seamless symphony, each step a testament to their unbreakable bond.

As they twirled and leaped across the stage, their eyes locked in a silent conversation, a melody of friendship resonating in their hearts. With every graceful motion, they wove a tapestry of emotions, each step bringing them closer together.

The strains of a poignant song about friendship enveloped the auditorium, its lyrics weaving through the air like a gentle embrace. Neel and Nitin moved in perfect harmony, their souls entwined in the music's embrace.

In a fleeting moment, their gazes met, and a shared smile blossomed between them. It was in that precious instant that they realized the depth of their connection, the profound truth that they were meant to dance through life together.

As the final chords of the song faded into silence, the audience erupted into a thunderous applause, their cheers a testament to the magic that Neel and Nitin had created on stage.

With their hands clasped tightly, Neel and Nitin bowed deeply, their hearts overflowing with gratitude for the bond they shared. For in that moment, they knew that no matter what the future held, they would always have each other, dancing through life hand in hand.

Neel's hand trembled with fury as he flung the first trophy out of the window, his voice a raw scream echoing through the room. "Dreaming with you was perhaps the biggest mistake of my life, Neel. Today, I understand that everything you did for me in this tuned life, you did for your own selfish reasons!"

His words hung heavy in the air, charged with a bitter sense of betrayal and disillusionment. With each trophy that followed, crashing against the unforgiving pavement below, Neel's rage burned brighter, fueled by the realization that the dreams they once shared were nothing but hollow promises.

In that moment of seething anger, Neel felt the weight of his shattered dreams pressing down on him, suffocating him with a sense of profound loss. Yet amidst the wreckage of broken trophies, a flicker of resolve ignited within him, a determination to forge a new path free from the shadows of false promises.

As the last trophy shattered against the ground, Neel stood in the silence that followed, his chest heaving with emotion. In that solitary moment, he made a silent vow to himself – to reclaim his dreams, to build a future on his own terms, and to never again allow himself to be deceived by false promises of friendship.

# Eternal Bonds

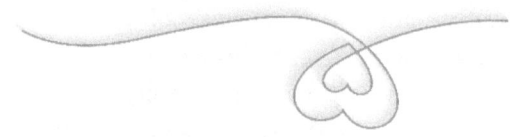

The balmy night air of Goa was heavy with the weight of Nitin's illness. He lay in bed, restless and feverish, while Neel sat by his side, concern etched deeply into his brow.

Neel gently placed a cold towel on Nitin's forehead, hoping to ease his discomfort. "Hang in there, Nitin. You'll feel better soon," he reassured, his voice laced with genuine concern.

Nitin weakly nodded, his eyes reflecting gratitude for Neel's unwavering support. "I don't know what I'd do without you, Neel," he murmured, his voice barely above a whisper.

Neel offered a reassuring smile, his heart heavy with worry for his friend. "You'll never have to find out, Nitin. I'll always be here for you," he vowed, his voice steady and comforting.

As the night wore on, Nitin's condition gradually improved. With Neel's constant care and support, he found solace in knowing he wasn't alone in his struggles.

Once Nitin felt well enough to move about, Neel suggested they take a stroll along the moonlit beach. The sound of the waves crashing against the shore provided a soothing backdrop to their conversation.

"I'm sorry for being such a burden, Neel," Nitin confessed, his voice tinged with regret. "You've done so much for me, and I don't know how to repay you."

Neel shook his head, his eyes reflecting understanding and compassion. "You don't owe me anything, Nitin. Friends take care of each other, no matter what," he replied, his voice filled with sincerity.

Their footsteps left imprints in the sand as they walked, the rhythm of their conversation flowing effortlessly between them. They spoke of shared memories and future dreams, finding comfort in each other's company.

As they reached the shoreline, Neel turned to Nitin with a soft smile. "Let's capture this moment," he suggested, pulling out his phone to take a selfie against the backdrop of the moonlit sea.

Nitin smiled weakly, but his eyes sparkled with gratitude. "Thank you, Neel. For everything," he said, his voice choked with emotion.

Neel wrapped an arm around Nitin's shoulder, pulling him into a warm embrace. "Anytime, Nitin. Anytime," he replied, his words carrying the weight of their unbreakable bond.

Together, they stood on the beach, watching as the waves crashed against the shore, knowing that no matter what challenges lay ahead, they would face them together, as friends.

As the night deepened, Neel and Nitin lay side by side on the beach, their bodies pressed against the warm sand, their souls entwined in conversation.

"I don't think anyone will ever love me as much as you do, Neel," Nitin confessed, his voice filled with vulnerability.

Neel turned to Nitin, his eyes reflecting unwavering affection. "And I don't think I'll ever find anyone who brings as much light into my life as you do," he replied, gently squeezing Nitin's hand.

In the quiet of the night, with the sound of the waves lulling them into a state of peace, Neel and Nitin shared a moment of profound connection. They knew that while many people would come and go in their lives, their bond was unbreakable, their friendship eternal.

The next morning, as the sun rose over the horizon, Neel and Nitin embarked on a journey that would forever mark their friendship. With determination and a shared sense of purpose, they made their way to a local tattoo parlor.

Side by side, they sat as the tattoo artist carefully etched the letters "NN" onto their wrists, a symbol of their unending friendship and the strength of their bond.

As they admired their new tattoos, Neel and Nitin exchanged a knowing smile, their hearts overflowing with gratitude for the journey they had embarked on together. With the sun shining down upon them, they knew that no matter what challenges lay ahead, they would face them with unwavering support and unconditional love for each other.

With a heavy heart, Neel traced his fingers over the tattoo on his wrist, his mind swirling with conflicting emotions. "This tattoo will remind me for a lifetime that friendship is nothing but an illusion," he muttered bitterly to himself.

Sitting on the edge of his bed, Neel reached for the burning cigarette in his trembling hand. Without a second thought, he pressed the glowing tip against the inked letters of the tattoo, the searing pain mirroring the turmoil within his soul.

As wisps of smoke curled around the charred edges of the tattoo, Neel felt a surge of anguish wash over him. Tears welled up in his eyes, mingling with the smoke as they cascaded down his cheeks.

"Pain begets pain," he whispered, his voice choked with emotion. "One day, I'll be free from this agony."

In that moment of raw vulnerability, Neel found solace in the physical pain inflicted upon his skin, a tangible manifestation of the emotional scars that ran deep within him. With each searing sensation, he hoped to numb the ache in his heart, longing for the day when the pain would no longer consume him.

# Fractured Bonds:
# A Tale of Lost Friendship

"Pallavi, meet me at the club. I'm booking a room for us," Nitin's voice echoed through the phone, heavy with the weight of his own choices. He knew he needed to drown out the turmoil within him tonight, seeking solace in the numbing embrace of alcohol, drugs, and fleeting encounters. With a sigh, he turned on the shower, hoping to wash away his troubles along with the suds.

"Neel, pass me the soap," Nitin called out, injecting a playful tone into his words as he envisioned their usual banter. Beneath the cascading water, he closed his eyes, attempting to find solace in the simple act of showering.

Neel, ever the faithful friend, bent down to retrieve the soap, a small smile playing on his lips as he anticipated their lighthearted exchange. As he reached out, Nitin's voice echoed in his mind, recalling a particular memory. "Remember that day, Neel? Remember what you did?" The memory sparked a chuckle from Nitin, a fond recollection of their shared antics.

Suddenly, the bathroom filled with laughter, a joyous symphony that reverberated off the tiled walls. Nitin and Neel joined in, their spirits lifted by the familiarity of their camaraderie. But in the midst of their mirth, Nitin's hand inadvertently struck the glass shower door with a resounding thud.

The laughter halted abruptly, replaced by a tense silence that hung heavily between them. Neel's gaze bore into Nitin's, reflecting a mixture of concern and regret, but Nitin turned away, unable to confront the weight of their shared history.

As the water continued to flow, washing away the evidence of their laughter and the stain of their unresolved conflicts, Nitin stood in silence, his heart heavy with unspoken truths. Each droplet seemed to echo the echoes of their past, reminding him of the bond they once shared and the fractures that had since formed.

In the privacy of the shower, Nitin grappled with the complexities of their relationship, unsure of how to bridge the gap that had widened between them. But as the steam enveloped him, obscuring his reflection in the mirror, he knew that he couldn't continue to avoid the truth forever.

---

In a dimly lit, overcrowded bar pulsating with music and laughter, Nitin finds himself lost in the rhythm of the night, his senses heightened by the heady combination of alcohol and adrenaline. Amidst the swirling chaos, he spots Pallavi, her eyes gleaming with mischief as she matches his steps on the dance floor.

As they sway to the music, Nitin's inhibitions melt away, and he leans in close to Pallavi, his voice barely audible above the din of the crowd.

Nitin: "Pallavi, I've never felt this way before. I love you."

Pallavi's laughter rings out melodiously, her words laced with playful affection.

Pallavi: "Oh Nitin, you're such a charmer! I love you too, silly."

Their banter continues as they navigate through the throngs of people, their laughter intertwining with the pulsating beats of the music. With each step, Nitin feels himself drawn closer to Pallavi, their connection growing stronger with every shared smile and stolen glance.

As the night wears on, Nitin leads Pallavi to a quieter corner of the bar, his touch lingering on her arm as they exchange knowing looks. Without a word, they slip away from the crowd, their footsteps echoing softly against the tiled floor as they make their way to a secluded room.

Behind closed doors, their passion ignites, their bodies moving in perfect harmony as they lose themselves in each other's embrace. In the intimate space, time seems to stand still as they explore the depths of their desires, their whispered confessions filling the air with a sense of longing and fulfillment.

Finally, spent from their ardor, they collapse onto the bed, their bodies entwined in a tangle of limbs and bedsheets. In the quiet aftermath, they find solace in each other's arms, their breaths slow and steady as they drift off to sleep, their hearts entwined in the silent promise of a love yet to unfold.

Nitin's sleepless night stretched on endlessly, the weight of his emotions pressing down on him like a suffocating blanket. He stood by the window, the moonlight casting eerie shadows across the room, his heart heavy with unspoken words and unresolved feelings.

"Why does my body feel content, but my soul remains empty?" he whispered into the silent darkness, the ache in his chest threatening to consume him whole. His thoughts drifted to Neel, his best friend, his confidant, the one person who had always understood him like no other.

"Why does no one else make me feel as safe as Neel does?" Nitin's voice trembled with raw emotion as tears welled up in his eyes, cascading down his cheeks like silent rivers of despair. "Why can't I open my heart to anyone else?"

The weight of his loneliness bore down on him, a suffocating burden that threatened to crush him beneath its weight. He buried his face in his hands, his body wracked with silent sobs as he grappled with overwhelming sense of loss and longing that consumed him.

"Neel, what have you taken from me that I didn't even realize?" he choked out, his words choked with pain and regret. His heart ached with a profound emptiness, a void that seemed impossible to fill.

As the night dragged on, Nitin's tears eventually subsided, but the ache in his heart remained, a constant reminder of the bond he had lost. He longed for the comfort and understanding that only Neel could provide, yet he couldn't bring himself to confront the depth of his emotions.

With a heavy heart, Nitin finally crawled back into bed beside Pallavi, but sleep continued to elude him. His mind buzzed with unanswered questions and unspoken feelings, leaving him feeling adrift in a sea of loneliness and despair.

……..,.,,

Pallavi's gentle touch on Nitin's shoulder sent a shiver down his spine, her presence a comforting anchor in the storm of his emotions. "Nitin, I know you still haven't forgotten Neel," she said softly, her voice a soothing balm to his troubled soul.

Nitin's jaw clenched, his eyes flashing with a mix of frustration and defiance. "No, Pallavi. You don't understand," he retorted sharply, his tone tinged with bitterness. "It's not about sexual preference. Neel and I share an emotional bond that transcends labels."

Pallavi sighed, her expression tinged with empathy as she tried to reach through the walls Nitin had erected around his heart. "Nitin, emotional attachment is not the same as physical attraction," she explained patiently, her words measured and gentle. "The connection you share with Neel is something that cannot be forced or denied."

"I hate him," Nitin snapped, his voice dripping with venom as he grappled with the conflicting emotions swirling within him.

Pallavi reached for her pack of cigarettes, her movements deliberate as she searched for the right words to comfort Nitin. "Nitin, you're drowning in hatred, but you're only fighting against yourself," she remarked, her voice tinged with concern. "You keep trying to push away your feelings, but you're only pushing yourself further into despair."

Frustrated and unable to confront the depth of his emotions, Nitin stormed out of the room, his heart heavy with unresolved feelings and the weight of his own inner turmoil. As he disappeared into the darkness, Pallavi could only watch helplessly, her heart aching for the pain he carried within him.

# NEEL

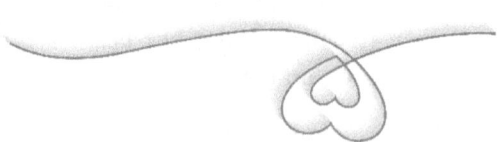

# Fractured Souls

Neil sat in silence, his mind swirling with conflicting emotions, as Richard's proposition lingered in the air like a heavy fog. The dimly lit bar provided a sanctuary for their conversation, the ambient noise of clinking glasses and distant chatter providing a backdrop to their inner turmoil.

Richard leaned forward, his expression softening with concern. "Neil, I can see the turmoil within you. You're carrying a heavy burden, my friend. But you don't have to face it alone."

Neil's gaze remained fixed on the table, his fingers tracing invisible patterns on the surface. "What do you know about me, Richard? You see the facade, but you don't know the depths of my struggles."

Richard reached out, placing a comforting hand on Neil's shoulder. "I may not know the specifics, but I can sense your pain. We all carry our burdens, Neil, but sharing them with others can lighten the load."

Neil's eyes flickered with a mixture of defiance and vulnerability. "I've built walls around myself for so long, Richard. Opening up feels like tearing them down brick by brick."

Richard nodded, his gaze unwavering. "Breaking down those walls can be terrifying, Neil. But it's also liberating. Vulnerability is not a weakness; it's a strength. It's what connects us to one another, what makes us human."

Neil's jaw clenched as he wrestled with his inner demons. "But what if I'm too broken to be fixed? What if I let someone in, only to hurt them in the end?"

Richard's voice was gentle yet firm. "We're all broken in some way, Neil. But it's through our brokenness that we find strength. And as for hurting others, that's a risk we all take when we open our hearts. But it's a risk worth taking for the chance at true connection."

Neil's shoulders sagged as the weight of his burdens threatened to crush him. "I don't know if I'm ready, Richard. The thought of facing my demons terrifies me."

Richard offered a reassuring smile. "You don't have to face them alone, Neil. I'll be here every step of the way, as will others who care about you. You're not as alone as you think."

Tears welled up in Neil's eyes as he finally allowed himself to release the pent-up emotions he had been holding back for so long. "Thank you, Richard. I don't know what I'd do without you."

Richard squeezed Neil's shoulder in a gesture of solidarity. "You'll never have to find out, my friend. We're in this together."

As the night wore on, Neil and Richard continued their conversation, delving deeper into the complexities of their shared humanity. With each word spoken, Neil felt the walls around his heart begin to crumble, allowing the light of connection to seep in.

In that moment, amidst the dimly lit bar and the cacophony of voices, Neil found solace in the knowledge that he was not alone. And with Richard by his side, he knew that he could face whatever demons lay ahead, armed with the strength of vulnerability and the power of human connection.

As Neil left the bar, a sense of peace washed over him. His steps were lighter, his heart a little less burdened. Yet, as he absentmindedly brushed his fingers over the nn tattoo on his wrist, a pang of guilt shot through him. Nitin's face flashed before his eyes, a constant reminder of the friend he had let down. Despite the progress he had made that night, Neil couldn't shake the feeling of responsibility that weighed heavily on his shoulders.

............

# Echoes of Friendship

Neil sat alone in his dimly lit room, the soft glow of the moon casting long shadows across the walls. With trembling hands, he reached for the wooden box tucked away in the corner, a repository of cherished memories and forgotten dreams.

As he lifted the lid, a rush of nostalgia washed over him, transporting him back to a time when life was simpler, when laughter filled the air and friendship knew no bounds. His fingers closed around a worn pencil, its once vibrant colors faded with time, but its significance undiminished by the passage of years.

In the flickering light of a candle, Neil's memories came alive, painting vivid images of their childhood adventures: climbing trees, building forts, and dreaming of a future filled with endless possibilities. But amidst the laughter and joy, there were moments of doubt and fear, moments when Neil questioned his own worthiness, his own ability to be the friend Nitin deserved.

Tears welled up in Neil's eyes as he remembered the pain of their parting, the bitter taste of regret that lingered long after Nitin had gone. He had let fear and insecurity drive a wedge between them, had allowed doubt to cloud his judgment and blind him to the true meaning of friendship.

But as Neil sat alone in the silence of his room, surrounded by the echoes of the past, he knew that it was not too late to mend what had been broken, to rebuild the bridges that had been burned. With a renewed sense of determination, he vowed to seek out Nitin, to make amends for the mistakes of the past and to reclaim the friendship that had once meant everything to him.

With trembling hands, Neil reached for a pen and a scrap of paper, his heart pouring out words of longing and regret, of hope and redemption. And as he penned a poem on the back of an old envelope, the words flowed freely, a testament to the enduring power of friendship:

In the tapestry of life, woven with care,

Two souls entwined, a bond beyond compare.

Through laughter and tears, through joy and strife,

Together we stand, bound by the thread of life.

Though storms may rage and darkness fall,

Our friendship shines, a beacon for all.

For in each other's arms, we find our light,

Guiding us through the darkest night.

And so we journey, hand in hand,

Through life's great tapestry, a wondrous land.

With every step, with every breath,

Our friendship grows, defying death.

For in the end, when all is said and done,

It is love that binds us, two hearts as one.

Forever and always, till the end of time,

Our friendship endures, a sacred chime.

As Neil's tears fell upon the paper, he remembered a time when he and Nitin had sat together, sharpening the same pencil from both ends, a symbol of their shared journey through life. They had laughed and joked, their voices mingling with the sound of scraping metal, as they talked about their hopes and dreams, their fears and insecurities.

"It's like our friendship, Neel," Nitin had said, his eyes shining with a mixture of joy and sadness. "No matter how many times we sharpen it, no matter how many times life tries to wear us down, we always come out stronger, more resilient than before."

With a sigh, Neil closed the lid of the wooden box, his mind filled with memories of a friendship that had weathered the storms of life and emerged stronger than ever. And as he drifted off to sleep, a sense of peace washed over him, knowing that no matter where life took him, no matter what challenges lay ahead, he would always carry the spirit of their friendship in his heart.

Early in the morning Neil sat alone in his room, his heart heavy with the weight of his memories of last

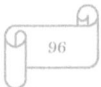

night With a mix of anticipation and trepidation, he reached once again for the wooden box tucked away in the corner. Its weathered exterior bore the scars of time, but within lay the remnants of a friendship he could never forget.

As he lifted the lid, a rush of emotions threatened to overwhelm him. Among the faded mementos and forgotten treasures, his fingers closed around a small pouch, its fabric worn and frayed with age. With a heavy heart, Neil emptied its contents onto the bed, the charred remnants of a cigarette scattering across the sheets.

With a deep sigh, Neil picked up one of the burnt butts, holding it between his fingers as if it were a fragile piece of glass. Memories flooded his mind, transporting him back to a time when he and Nitin had shared laughter and dreams, when the world had seemed full of endless possibilities.

"Nitin, these are the cigarettes we used to smoke together," Neil whispered, his voice barely audible in the silence of the room. "Even now, when I hold them in my hands, I can feel the warmth of your touch, the sound of your laughter echoing in my ears. It's not just your body I miss, Nitin, it's your presence, your essence that lingers on."

Tears welled up in Neil's eyes as he spoke, his heart heavy with longing and regret. "I'm handing over my body to Richard, but I'll never give up my heart, my feelings. That first and last time you made me yours, that feeling can never be taken away from me."

With a trembling hand, Neil brought the cigarette butt to his lips, inhaling deeply as if trying to capture the essence of his lost friend. The bitter taste of smoke filled his mouth, mingling with the salt of his tears as he closed his eyes and let the memories wash over him.

"Nitin," he whispered, his voice barely a whisper. "I'm sorry for everything, for all the pain I've caused you. I miss you more than words can say, and I'll carry your memory with me always, like a precious treasure hidden deep within my heart."

And as Neil sat alone in the darkness, his tears mingling with the ashes of the past, he knew that no matter where life took him, no matter what trials lay ahead, the bond he shared with Nitin would always remain unbreakable, a beacon of hope in the darkness of his soul.

Suddenly neils eyes fell upon something unexpected— a condom. Amidst tears and laughter, he reminisced about the day Nitin had nervously prepared for his first date.

Nitin: "Neil, I'm really scared, man."

Neil: "Why, what's wrong?"

Nitin: "It's my first time, you know. What if something goes wrong?"

Neil: "Come on, we've aced our twelfth grade and watched enough movies to know what to do."

Nitin, pulling over the car: "Neil, please, get a condom."

Neil, smiling: "Oh, come on, what's the big deal?"

Nitin: "Just get two."

Neil: "Oh, what's up with you, Nitin?"

Nitin: "One's for you."

Neil: "For me?"

Nitin: "Who knows, maybe you'll need it with her friend. laughs"

The night hung heavy with the weight of expectations as Neil watched Nitin disappear into the depths of the house with Riya, leaving him alone with his thoughts. Neil knew what awaited Nitin and Riya behind the closed door—a night of intimacy, a night of shared secrets, a night of love.

As the hours ticked by, Neil found himself drowning in a sea of alcohol and smoke, trying to numb the pain that gnawed at his heart. Each sip of whiskey burned his throat, each puff of smoke clouded his mind, but nothing could extinguish the fire of jealousy and longing that raged within him.

Outside, the world was silent, but inside, Neil's mind was a whirlwind of emotions. He replayed every moment he had shared with Nitin—their laughter, their tears, their secrets. He remembered the warmth of Nitin's embrace, the sparkle in his eyes, the sound of his laughter that once filled the room with joy.

But now, all Neil could hear was the deafening silence of the empty room, echoing the emptiness in his heart. He longed to reach out to Nitin, to hold him close and never let go, but he knew that Nitin belonged to someone else now, someone who could give him the love and happiness he deserved.

As the night stretched on, Neil's vision blurred, his mind clouded with memories of happier times. He stumbled to his feet, the room spinning around him, and collapsed onto the floor in a drunken stupor. Tears streamed down his cheeks, mingling with the whiskey and smoke, as he whispered Nitin's name into the darkness.

Hours passed, but Neil remained trapped in his own personal hell, tormented by thoughts of Nitin and Riya together, sharing a bed, sharing a life. He cursed himself for ever letting Nitin slip through his fingers, for never having the courage to tell him how he truly felt.

But as the first light of dawn crept through the curtains, Neil's resolve hardened. He knew that he could no longer live in the shadow of his own insecurities, that he had to find the strength to let go of Nitin and move on with his life.

With a heavy heart, Neil gathered his belongings and made his way to the door, leaving behind the ghosts of the past and stepping into a future filled with uncertainty. But as he walked out into the cool morning air, he felt a glimmer of hope flicker within him—a hope that one day, he would find the courage to love again.

As Neil stood there, grappling with his emotions, Nitin's words cut through the air like a knife. The weight of their shared history bore down on him, and for a moment, Neil felt as though the walls were closing in around him.

"Idiot, where are you going? We haven't even talked about what happened. Your condom was used," Nitin's voice rang out, filled with a mix of concern and frustration.

Neil's head hung low, unable to meet Nitin's gaze. "Yes," he murmured, his voice barely above a whisper.

Without another word, Nitin took Neil by the hand and led him back into the room. They lay down side by side, the silence between them heavy with unspoken words and unresolved emotions.

The night passed in a blur, sleep eluding them both as they lay there, lost in their own thoughts. Neil couldn't shake the image of Nitin and Riya together, their laughter echoing in his mind like a cruel taunt.

Nitin, sensing Neil's turmoil, pulled him close, wrapping him in a comforting embrace. "You know, Neil, if I ever try to leave, don't let me. Promise me," Nitin whispered, his voice thick with emotion.

Neil's heart ached at Nitin's words, the depth of their friendship laid bare in that moment. "I promise," he replied, his voice choked with tears.

As they lay there, Neil watched Nitin drift off to sleep, his chest rising and falling in a steady rhythm. He couldn't help but feel a surge of protectiveness towards his friend, a fierce determination to never let him go.

Gently, Neil pressed his lips to Nitin's forehead, whispering softly, "I can't leave you, Nitin. I'll never leave you."

Nitin, stirred from his slumber by Neil's touch, pulled him closer, his arms wrapping around Neil's trembling

form. "With you, Neil, I can finally sleep peacefully," he murmured, his voice filled with gratitude.

But Neil's heart clenched at Nitin's words, the weight of his promise heavy upon him. "If you ever leave, Neil, just remember, I'll never sleep peacefully again," Nitin whispered, his words a solemn vow.

, Neil knew that no matter what the future held, their bond would endure. For in the quiet moments between them, in the unspoken words and shared memories, lay the true strength of their friendship

# Echoes of Solitude

Neel steps out of the bathroom, the warmth of the water failing to penetrate the icy grip of loneliness that clutches at his heart. Each step he takes is heavy with the weight of his thoughts, echoing in the empty silence of his apartment. He opens his wardrobe, only to find it half-filled with clothes and half-empty, a poignant reminder of the shared life he once had with Nitin. The sight of the empty hangers tugs at Neel's heart, each one a silent testament to the void that now consumes him.

As he moves to the shoe rack, Neel can't help but feel a pang of sadness at the sight of the sparse collection of footwear. Once filled with the vibrant colors and styles that mirrored their shared zest for life, the rack now stands as a testament to the absence that looms large in Neel's life. Each pair of shoes holds memories of moments shared with Nitin, now nothing more than painful reminders of what once was.

On the breakfast table, two plates await him, the contrast between them a poignant reminder of the loneliness that now defines his existence. One sits empty, adorned with a single red rose and a card bearing Nitin's name, a silent welcome back that only serves to deepen the ache in Neel's heart. The other holds Neel's breakfast, but the food seems tasteless and unappetizing in the face of his overwhelming grief. Each bite is a struggle, the simple act of eating a painful reminder of the void left by Neel's absence.

As Neel sits alone at the breakfast table, the weight of his loneliness pressing down on him like a suffocating blanket, he can't help but long for the warmth and companionship he once shared with Nitin . The emptiness of his surroundings serves as a constant reminder of the void in his life, a void that seems impossible to fill. And as he stares at the empty plate before him, his heart heavy with sorrow, Neil can't shake the feeling that he has lost more than just a friend—he has lost a part of himself.

Neil picks up his phone and dials Richard's number, his hand trembling with the weight of his emotions. "Richard," he begins, his voice thick with emotion, "I… I can't do this. I can't let you move in with me. There's no space left in my home or my heart for anyone else. We can spend nights together, but life… life is something else," Neel's voice cracks with the weight of his words, the ache of his loneliness echoing through the phone line.

Richard listens quietly, his heart heavy with empathy as he hears the pain in Neel's voice. "Neel, I understand," he replies softly, his own voice tinged with sadness. "But you can't keep shutting yourself off from the world. It's okay to grieve, but you have to remember that life goes on. You can't let your past consume your present."

Neel's eyes fill with tears as he listens to Richard's words, the truth of his friend's advice cutting through the fog of his despair. "But how do I move on, Richard?" he asks, his voice trembling with uncertainty. "How do I let go of the one person who meant everything to me?"

Richard sighs, his heart aching for his friend's pain. "Neel, moving on doesn't mean forgetting Nitin or what you had together," he explains gently. "It means finding a way to honor his memory while still living your own life. It means allowing yourself to open up to new experiences and new relationships, even if it feels impossible right now."

As Neel hangs up the phone, he sinks into a chair at the table, the empty seat across from him a painful reminder of what once was. He stares at the rose on the empty plate, its vibrant red petals a stark contrast to the emptiness that now surrounds him.

Tears well up in Neel's eyes as he realizes the depth of his loss. The absence of Nitin's laughter, his warmth, his presence—it's like a gaping hole in Neel's soul, one that he's not sure will ever be filled again.

But amidst the pain and the emptiness, Neil finds a glimmer of hope. Maybe, just maybe, one day the emptiness will fade, and he'll find solace in the memories of the love they shared. Until then, he'll carry on, one empty day at a time, longing for the warmth of Nitin's embrace to fill the void in his heart.

And as he sits alone in his empty apartment, Neel makes a silent vow to himself—to honor Nitin's memory by living his life to the fullest, even if it means facing the pain of their separation head-on. He may be alone for now, but he knows that he's not truly alone as long as he carries Nitin's love with him in his heart.

# Behind the Smile

As the lecture wound down, a student raised her hand tentatively, her eyes shining with admiration. Neel nodded, inviting her to speak.

"Professor Neel, I just want to say that I've always been a huge fan of your and Nitin's work together," she began, her voice filled with sincerity. "The songs you wrote, the music and dance you both composed together—it's all so incredibly beautiful and moving. I've often wondered why you two parted ways. Your collaboration seemed magical."

Neel's expression softened at her words, a bittersweet smile playing on his lips. He took a moment to collect his thoughts before responding.

"Thank you for your kind words," he said, his voice tinged with a hint of sadness. "Nitin and I shared a special bond, both personally and creatively. Our partnership yielded some of the most meaningful work of my career."

Pausing for a moment, Neel's gaze drifted to a distant memory, his mind filled with images of laughter, late-night jam sessions, and heartfelt conversations.

"But life has a way of leading us down different paths," he continued, his tone somber. "Sometimes, circumstances change, and we find ourselves walking alone, yearning for the familiarity and comfort of the past."

A heavy silence settled over the room as Neel's words lingered in the air, the weight of his unspoken grief palpable to all who listened. Despite his attempts to maintain composure, the pain of separation still cut deep, a constant reminder of what once was.

The student nodded understandingly, her eyes reflecting compassion and empathy. "Thank you for sharing that with us, Professor Neel," she said softly. "Your honesty and vulnerability inspire us all."

Neel offered her a grateful smile, touched by her empathy. In that moment, he realized that perhaps, despite the distance and pain, there was solace to be found in the connections forged through shared experiences and shared sorrow.

As Neel listened to the student's heartfelt words, a sense of gratitude washed over him. With a gentle nod, he acknowledged her observation before addressing the class as a whole.

"You know," Neel began, his voice carrying a sense of introspection, "pain has a peculiar way of seeping into our lives, shaping our experiences, and often finding its way into our art."

The room fell silent, every student leaning in to catch his words, their curiosity piqued by his insight.

"It's true," Neel continued, his gaze sweeping across the room. "In moments of joy, we may find inspiration, but it's in moments of pain—of heartache and longing—that our art truly comes alive. It's as if every hurt, every tear shed, becomes a brushstroke on the canvas of our souls."

A murmur of agreement rippled through the room, students nodding in understanding as they absorbed Neel's wisdom.

"Pain adds depth to our creations," Neel went on, his voice growing more animated with each word. "It infuses them with raw emotion, with a rawness and authenticity that can't be replicated. It's what makes our art resonate with others, what makes it speak to the human experience in ways that words alone cannot."

As Neel spoke, he felt a sense of clarity wash over him, a newfound understanding of the role pain played in his own creative journey. Despite the hardships and heartaches he had endured, he realized that each one had contributed to the richness and depth of his art, shaping him into the artist he was today.

"And so, my dear students," Neel concluded, his voice ringing with conviction, "embrace your pain, for it is a gift—a catalyst for growth, for transformation, and ultimately, for the creation of something truly extraordinary."

With those words, he left his students to ponder the profound truth he had shared, a flicker of hope igniting within each of them as they contemplated the power of pain in their own lives and art.

As Neel exits the lecture room, the students gather in small groups, their voices hushed as they discuss their favorite teacher and the enigma that surrounds him.

"He's always so cheerful and positive," one student remarks, admiration evident in her voice. "But I can't shake the feeling that there's something he's not telling us."

Her friend nods in agreement, a thoughtful expression on her face. "I've noticed that too. It's like he's hiding something behind that smile of his."

As they continue to talk, more students join the conversation, each sharing their own observations and theories about Neel's mysterious demeanor. Some speculate about his personal life, while others wonder if he's facing some sort of internal struggle.

"He's always there for us, no matter what," another student chimes in, her voice tinged with gratitude. "But I wish he'd let us in a little more. It feels like he's carrying the weight of the world on his shoulders."

The conversation grows more emotional as the students reflect on the impact Neel has had on their lives. They recount moments of kindness and encouragement, each one a testament to the depth of Neel's character.

"He's more than just a teacher," one student declares, her voice filled with conviction. "He's a mentor, a friend, someone who truly cares about us."

As the bell rings, signaling the end of the discussion, the students disperse, each one carrying with them a renewed sense of appreciation for the man who has touched their lives in ways they may never fully understand. And as they go about their day, they can't help but wonder what lies behind Neel's infectious smile, and if they'll ever uncover the truth hidden within.

# Drifting Tides

As Neel strolled along the serene seashore, the rhythmic sound of crashing waves providing a soothing backdrop, his thoughts drifted to happier times. He paused, a nostalgic smile gracing his lips, as he watched two children playing in the sand, their laughter echoing in the salty breeze.

For a fleeting moment, Neel's heart swelled with warmth as he imagined himself and Nitin in their younger days, carefree and unburdened by the weight of adulthood. He could almost hear their playful banter and feel the sand between his toes as they chased each other along the shore.

But then, without warning, a powerful wave surged forth, engulfing one of the children and dragging them into the churning sea. Neel's heart clenched in terror as he watched the scene unfold before him, his breath catching in his throat.

Instinct took over as Neel sprinted towards the water, his pulse pounding in his ears. Without hesitation, he plunged into the icy depths, the frigid water enveloping him in its embrace. Desperation fueled his movements as he reached out, his fingers grasping desperately for his friend's hand.

"Nitin!" Neel cried out, his voice raw with fear and anguish. "Hold on, I've got you!"

With every fiber of his being, Neel fought against the relentless pull of the ocean, his muscles straining with the effort. He refused to let go, refusing to accept the possibility of losing his friend to the unforgiving sea.

As Nitin's fingers slipped from his grasp, Neel's heart plummeted into the abyss of despair. Tears mingled with the saltwater as he struggled to keep his head above the surface, his mind flooded with memories of their shared laughter and joy.

But just as all hope seemed lost, a strong hand gripped Neel's wrist, pulling him to safety. Gasping for breath, Neel collapsed onto the shore, his body wracked with exhaustion and relief.

"Thank you," Nitin whispered, his voice barely audible over the roar of the waves. "I thought I was a goner."

Neel's eyes met Nitin's, a silent understanding passing between them. In that moment, they were no longer just friends—they were survivors, bound together by a bond that transcended time and tide.

As they lay on the sandy shore, their hearts still racing with adrenaline, Neel felt a sense of gratitude wash over him. Despite the dangers that lurked beneath the surface, he knew that as long as they had each other, they could weather any storm that came their way.

As Neel lay on the shore, the weight of their near-tragedy sinking in, his thoughts drifted to the uncertain future that lay ahead. The realization hit him like a crashing wave – in a world filled with turmoil and chaos, could he and Nitin navigate the challenges alone?

A pang of fear gripped Neel's heart as he considered the possibility of facing life's trials without Nitin by his side. They had always been each other's pillars of strength, their bond unbreakable even in the face of adversity. But now, with the tides of fate pulling them in different directions, Neel couldn't shake the nagging doubt that lingered within him.

Closing his eyes, Neel offered up a silent prayer to the heavens above. "Please, God," he whispered fervently, "grant us the strength to weather whatever storms may come our way. And if ever Nitin finds himself in trouble, let me be there to share his sorrow, to offer him solace in his darkest hour."

As Neel sat alone on the shore, his mind consumed by the events that had just unfolded, a profound sense of solitude washed over him. In the quiet solitude of the beach, with only the sound of the waves breaking against the shore for company, Neel couldn't help but ponder the uncertain future that lay ahead.

His thoughts drifted to Nitin, his steadfast companion through the trials and tribulations of life. Would they ever reunite, he wondered, or had the currents of fate pulled them too far apart? And if they did find their way back to each other, would time and distance erode the bonds of their friendship, leaving them mere shadows of the inseparable duo they once were?

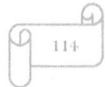

With a heavy heart and a soul weighed down by uncertainty, Neel gazed out at the vast expanse of the sea, searching for answers in the ebb and flow of the tides. But amidst the vastness of the ocean, he found only silence, a stark reminder of the unanswered questions that haunted his restless mind.

NITIN

# Echoes of the Muse

The National Awards ceremony was a spectacle to behold, a dazzling display of talent and artistry that left the audience spellbound. As Nitin stepped onto the stage to accept his award, the crowd erupted into thunderous applause, their admiration for his work evident in their fervent cheers.

The anchor, eager to delve into the intricacies of Nitin's choreography, posed a question that cut to the core of his creative process. "Nitin, your choreography in this song touched the hearts of millions. Can you share with us the inspiration behind it?"

Nitin's expression softened as he reflected on the question, memories of the past flooding his mind. "It was a moment of vulnerability," he admitted, his voice tinged with emotion. "A moment when I felt the weight of my own loneliness bearing down on me."

The anchor leaned in, captivated by Nitin's response. "Loneliness? How did you channel that into your choreography?"

Nitin paused, gathering his thoughts before responding. "I believe that art is a reflection of our innermost emotions," he explained. "In that moment of loneliness, I channeled my pain and longing into the movements, infusing them with a sense of depth and raw emotion."

As Nitin accepted the award from the President, there was a sense of pride and accomplishment that radiated from him. But beneath the surface, there was a lingering sense of melancholy, a silent acknowledgment of the absence that loomed over him.

The anchor, sensing Nitin's introspective mood, pressed further. "Nitin, you mentioned feeling alone in that moment. Is there someone special who inspired this choreography?"

Nitin's gaze drifted to the empty seat beside him, a pang of sadness washing over him. "Yes," he replied softly, his voice barely above a whisper. "Someone who was once my partner in both life and art."

The anchor nodded, a sympathetic understanding passing between them. "It sounds like this person played a significant role in your life."

Nitin nodded, his eyes betraying a hint of sorrow. "We were more than just a partner," he admitted. "He was my muse, my inspiration. And even though he is no longer by my side, his influence continues to shape my work."

As the ceremony drew to a close and Nitin stepped off the stage, a sense of longing lingered in his heart. Despite the accolades and recognition, he couldn't shake the feeling of emptiness that gnawed at him. But amidst the applause and adulation, there was a glimmer of

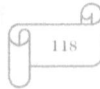

hope—a belief that perhaps, one day, he would find solace in the memories of the past and the promise of the future.

# Fractured Bonds

As Nitin crossed the threshold into his office, his heart clenched at the sight that greeted him. The door, once a barrier to the outside world, now stood ajar, a silent testament to the intrusion upon his sacred space. His eyes narrowed with a mixture of anger and sorrow as he confronted the unexpected trespassers attempting to remove his and Neel's life-size photograph.

"Who gave you the right to enter here?" Nitin's voice rang out, the tremble barely contained as he confronted the unwelcome visitors.

His mother's presence offered a sliver of solace amidst the turmoil, her gaze filled with empathy as she sat on the couch. Yet, Nitin couldn't help but feel a surge of frustration at her inability to shield their shared sanctuary from violation.

"Why?" Nitin's voice cracked, the pain in his heart threatening to spill over into the room.

Her explanation about vastu, well-intentioned though it may have been, felt like a dagger twisting in his already wounded heart. The room, once a bastion of shared dreams and aspirations with Neel, now stood as a desecrated shrine to their shattered bond.

"No, Mom, never. This room belongs to us, to our memories. No one else can lay claim to it," Nitin declared, his voice resonating with defiance.

But beneath the veneer of strength lay a torrent of grief, each corner of the room a silent witness to the depth of their estrangement. The remnants of their past whispered of what could have been, haunting Nitin with memories of a bond now fractured beyond repair.

As Nitin traced the contours of his tattoo, the inked memories etched into his skin, he couldn't help but feel the raw ache of longing for Neel's presence. The room bore witness to their shared dreams and aspirations, now reduced to mere shadows of a connection once cherished.

"Please, Mom, keep the door between our offices open. Let it serve as a bridge between us. But this room, this sacred space, must remain untouched by anyone else, regardless of any supposed vastu considerations," Nitin implored, his voice trembling with unspoken anguish.

With a silent understanding, his mother nodded, her eyes mirroring the depth of his pain. As Nitin turned to leave, the weight of their separation pressed heavily upon him, a constant reminder of the void that now resided in his heart.

As Nitin sat in his office, consumed by the turmoil of emotions swirling within him, he couldn't shake the relentless grip of memories tethered to Neel. The cigarette burned between his lips, its smoke mingling with his thoughts as he grappled with the question that plagued his restless mind: Why couldn't he move on, despite harboring so much resentment towards Neel?

With a heavy heart, Nitin pressed the burning tip of the cigarette against his lips, seeking solace in the pain it inflicted. "Where do I find those cigarettes that carry the sensation of your touch?" he murmured to himself, the bitterness of his words underscored by the ache of longing in his voice. He attempted to extinguish both the smoke and Neel's memory, but they stubbornly persisted, haunting him at every turn.

Driven by a relentless yearning, Nitin rose from his chair and made his way to Neel's deserted office. As he settled into Neel's chair and opened the drawer, his eyes fell upon a photograph—a poignant reminder of their fractured bond. "Why couldn't Neel leave a piece of himself behind for me to cling to, to ease the burden of my solitary existence?" Nitin whispered, his voice thick with unshed tears.

His fingers traced the contours of their intertwined figures in the photograph, each touch a bittersweet caress laden with unresolved emotions. The image, a silent testament to their shared past, served as a painful reminder of the chasm that now separated them.

As Nitin gazed upon the photograph, his heart weighed down by the weight of his longing, he realized that even in his absence, Neel continued to hold sway over his thoughts and emotions. The ache of their fractured friendship gnawed at Nitin's soul, leaving him adrift in a sea of regret and sorrow.

Lost in the labyrinth of his own emotions, Nitin's mind became a battleground, torn between resentment and yearning. With trembling hands, he reached for another cigarette, the sharp scent of smoke mingling with the lingering essence of Neel's presence in the room. Each puff was a futile attempt to drown out the echoes of their shared laughter and camaraderie, now swallowed by the deafening silence that enveloped him.

But amidst the haze of smoke and memories, Nitin found himself grappling with a profound sense of emptiness—a void that no amount of distraction could fill. His heart, burdened by the weight of unanswered questions and unresolved emotions, longed for closure, for a chance to make sense of the fractured pieces of their friendship.

As he stared at the photograph before him, Nitin was overcome by a surge of raw emotion—a tidal wave of grief and longing crashing against the shores of his soul. The image, frozen in time, captured a fleeting moment of happiness that now felt like a distant dream, a relic of a bond that had once been unbreakable.

With a heavy sigh, Nitin closed his eyes, allowing himself to be engulfed by the memories that threatened to consume him whole. In the quiet solitude of Neel's office, he found himself confronting the painful truth that despite their estrangement, a part of him would always belong to Neel, forever tethered to him by the invisible threads of their shared past.

And as the tears welled up in his eyes, tracing silent pathways down his cheeks, Nitin realized that perhaps the greatest tragedy of all was not the loss of their friendship, but the absence of closure—a wound that continued to fester, refusing to heal.

# Fragmented Reflections

The ambiance of the restaurant seemed to dim as Pallavi's words sliced through Nitin's defenses, laying bare the tumult that raged within his soul. He took a gulp of his wine, its bitterness a stark contrast to the turmoil brewing within him.

"Pallavi, you don't understand," Nitin began, his voice tinged with desperation.

"No, Nitin, you're the one who refuses to understand," Pallavi countered, her tone gentle yet unwavering. "That night, whatever transpired, it was natural. You could have halted it if you'd wished. But you didn't, because deep down, you craved that moment as much as Neel did. The difference lies in Neel's acceptance of that truth, while you're hell-bent on evading it."

Nitin's jaw tensed, his frustration bubbling to the surface. "You think I wanted that? You think I wanted to betray Neel and destroy our friendship?"

Pallavi reached out to touch his hand, her gaze softening with empathy. "No, Nitin, that's not what I'm saying. I know you didn't intend for things to unfold the way they did. But sometimes, our desires and actions don't align. And instead of facing that truth, you're burying yourself in denial."

Nitin pulled his hand away, his eyes flashing with defiance. "You don't know what it's like, Pallavi. You don't know the guilt and shame I carry every day."

Pallavi leaned in closer, her voice gentle yet firm. "I may not know your exact pain, Nitin, but I know what it's like to carry burdens and regrets. And I also know that healing begins with acceptance, not avoidance."

Nitin's shoulders slumped, the weight of Pallavi's words settling upon him like a leaden shroud. He knew she was right, but the prospect of facing his inner demons was daunting.

"Pallavi, I'm scared," Nitin admitted, his voice barely above a whisper. "I'm scared of what I might find if I delve too deep."

Pallavi reached out once more, her touch a soothing balm against his turmoil. "I know, Nitin. But I'll be here every step of the way. You don't have to face this alone."

As Nitin met Pallavi's gaze, he felt a glimmer of hope flicker within him. Maybe, just maybe, he could find the courage to confront his inner turmoil and emerge stronger on the other side.

"Pallavi, will you marry me?" Nitin's voice quivered with uncertainty, his heart laid bare before her.

Pallavi's eyes shimmered with empathy as she clasped his trembling hand in hers. "Nitin, I understand your pain, but marriage isn't a solution to your turmoil. We both know that your heart still belongs to Neel."

Nitin recoiled as if struck, his gaze falling to the tablecloth in shame. "I… I just thought…"

Pallavi squeezed his hand gently, her touch a balm to his wounded soul. "Nitin, I care for you deeply, but I won't be a substitute for what you truly desire. I can't be."

Tears welled in Nitin's eyes as he struggled to find the words to convey the depth of his emotions. "I know I can't give you the love you deserve. But please, Pallavi, be patient with me. I'm trying to find my way back to myself."

Pallavi's heart ached for him, her own tears glistening as she enveloped him in a tender embrace.

"Pallavi, I feel like I'm drowning," Nitin confessed, his voice barely audible above the din of the restaurant.

Pallavi leaned in closer, her eyes reflecting his pain. "Nitin, you're not alone. I'm here for you, always."

"But how can you understand what I'm going through?" Nitin's voice trembled with emotion, his vulnerability laid bare.

Pallavi reached out, gently brushing aside a stray lock of hair from his forehead. "Because I've seen the torment in your eyes, felt the weight of your sorrow. I may not know the depth of your pain, but I'm here to share the burden, if you'll let me."

Nitin's breath caught in his throat, the walls he had built around his heart crumbling in the face of Pallavi's unwavering compassion. "I don't know if I can ever let go of the past," he admitted, his voice heavy with regret.

Pallavi squeezed his hand reassuringly. "You don't have to let go, Nitin. But you can't let it consume you either. There's a whole world out there waiting for you to embrace it, if you're willing to take the first step."

Nitin's eyes glistened with unshed tears as he met Pallavi's gaze, a flicker of hope igniting within him. "Thank you, Pallavi. For being my anchor in the storm."

Pallavi smiled softly, her heart swelling with affection. "Anytime, Nitin. Anytime."

As they parted, Nitin watched Pallavi's graceful exit, a profound sense of gratitude washing over him for her unwavering support. In that moment, he realized the true value of friendship—the beacon of light that guided him through the darkest of storms. And though his path ahead remained uncertain, he took solace in the knowledge that Pallavi would be there, a steadfast companion in his journey of healing and self-discovery.

# Echoes of Longing

Nitin's mother gently placed her hand on Pallavi's, her expression filled with concern. "Pallavi, don't you think you're making a big mistake by saying yes to this marriage?"

"No, Aunty, I know Nitin won't be able to go through with this marriage. In fact, he won't be able to marry any girl. No matter what he says, he can never replace Neel in his life," Pallavi replied, her smile tinged with sadness as she signaled to the waiter.

"Pallavi, I know how stubborn my son can be. He can go to any extent to prove himself right," Nitin's mother said, stirring her coffee with a sugar cube.

"It's okay. If Neel loses, then I win," Pallavi's eyes reflected a hint of melancholy.

"But spending your entire life with someone without love is very difficult," Nitin's mother sighed heavily.

"Mother, if Nitin gives me even a fraction of the love he has for Neel, it's enough for me," Pallavi's smile was bittersweet.

Nitin's mother leaned in closer, her voice trembling with emotion. "Pallavi, my son is lost without Neel. I see the pain in his eyes every day, and it breaks my heart. I don't want to see him suffer anymore."

Pallavi reached out and gently squeezed Nitin's mother's hand, her eyes filled with empathy. "Aunty, I understand. But I also see the love he holds for Neel. It's a bond that's impossible to break, no matter how hard he tries."

Tears welled up in Nitin's mother's eyes as she spoke. "I just want him to be happy, Pallavi. But I fear that he'll never find happiness without Neel by his side."

Pallavi nodded, her own eyes moist with unshed tears. "I promise you, Aunty, I'll do everything in my power to make him happy. Even if it means sacrificing my own happiness."

Nitin's mother placed a comforting hand on Pallavi's shoulder, her voice choked with emotion. "You're a blessing, Pallavi. If anyone can bring joy back into my son's life, it's you."

As they sat in the coffee shop, surrounded by the gentle hum of conversation and the aroma of freshly brewed coffee, Pallavi and Nitin's mother found strength in each other's presence. They knew that the road ahead would be filled with challenges and heartache, but they also knew that their love and support for Nitin would see them through any storm.

"Whatever you kids decide, let me know so I can prepare everything," Nitin's mother said, her tone resigned yet supportive.

The coffee shop seemed to echo with the weight of their conversation, each word carrying the burden of unspoken emotions and silent sacrifices. In that moment, Pallavi and Nitin's mother found solace in each other's company, bound together by their shared understanding of the complexities of love and the sacrifices it often demands.

The soft glow of the dining room lights cast a warm ambiance as Nitin and his mother sat down for dinner, the clinking of cutlery the only sound breaking the comfortable silence.

"Nitin, I heard you proposed to Pallavi," his mother remarked casually, her eyes studying him intently.

Nitin nodded, a tentative smile playing on his lips. "Yes, Mom. Aren't you happy for me?" he asked, hoping for her approval.

His mother's expression remained impassive as she probed further. "Are you sure about this decision, Nitin? Do you love Pallavi the way you loved Neel?"

Nitin's brow furrowed in frustration. "Mom, I've explained this before. My relationship with Neel was different. We were friends, not lovers. Pallavi and I are a couple," he explained, his tone tinged with irritation.

His mother's next question struck a nerve. "Can't two people of the same sexuality be a couple?" she asked pointedly, her gaze unwavering.

Nitin's patience wore thin as he shot back, "Mom, I know where this conversation is headed. Neel and I were never a couple, and we never will be. I'm sorted about my relationships."

His mother couldn't help but chuckle at his defensiveness. "You? Sorted about relationships?" she teased, her tone light yet tinged with sadness. "You're the last person who can claim to be sorted, Nitin. Especially now that the one person who could knock some sense into you isn't here."

Nitin's temper flared at her words, his frustration boiling over as he slammed his fist on the table. "Don't talk about Neel like that!" he shouted, his voice laced with pain and anger.

His mother reached out, her touch gentle yet firm as she tried to calm him down. "Nitin, I'm sorry. I didn't mean to upset you," she said softly, her eyes filled with remorse.

As the tension dissipated, Nitin took a deep breath, his emotions still raw and raw. "If you're worried about Pallavi and me, Mom, I assure you, I'm doing this because I want to," he said quietly, his voice tinged with uncertainty.

His mother smiled warmly, her heart heavy with unspoken understanding. "Then I'll be happy for you, Nitin. Just promise me you'll take care of yourself," she replied, her words carrying a weight of love and concern.

As they finished their meal in silence, each lost in their own thoughts, Nitin couldn't help but wonder if his mother was right. Was he truly sorted about his relationships, or was he just fooling himself? And as he glanced at the empty seat across from him, a pang of longing pierced his heart, a silent reminder of the void left by Neel's absence.

Their conversation continued late into the night, the air thick with unspoken emotions and unresolved tensions. Nitin struggled to articulate his feelings, his words failing him in the face of his mother's probing questions.

"Mom, I just don't understand why you can't accept Pallavi as my partner," Nitin confessed, his voice tinged with frustration. "She's been there for me through everything, and I love her."

His mother sighed, her gaze softening as she reached out to grasp his hand. "Nitin, it's not about Pallavi. It's about you," she explained gently. "I want to make sure you're making the right decision for yourself, not just because you feel pressured to move on."

Nitin bristled at her words, his defenses rising instinctively. "I'm not being pressured, Mom. I love Pallavi, and I want to spend the rest of my life with her," he insisted, his voice growing more adamant.

His mother's expression softened, a hint of sadness flickering in her eyes. "I know you believe that, Nitin. But sometimes, love can blind us to the truth," she said softly. "I just want you to be happy, whatever that may look like."

Their conversation stretched long into the night, each revelation and confession laying bare the complexities of Nitin's heart. And as the hours ticked by, he couldn't help but feel a sense of gratitude for his mother's unwavering support, even in the face of his stubbornness and defiance.

As they finally retired to bed, the weight of their conversation still heavy on their minds, Nitin couldn't shake the feeling that his mother was right. Perhaps, in his quest to move on, he had overlooked the true depths of his own heart. And as he drifted off to sleep, his dreams filled with visions of Neel and Pallavi, he couldn't help but wonder if he would ever find the answers he sought.

# Ashes of Echoes

As Nitin sat in his office, the weight of his decisions bearing down on him, he couldn't shake the feeling of unease that gnawed at his heart. With a heavy sigh, he made a decision that he hoped would bring closure to the chapter of his life that revolved around Neel.

"Open Neel's office," Nitin instructed his assistant, his voice tinged with determination.

The air seemed to grow heavy as the door to Neel's office creaked open, revealing a space frozen in time, filled with memories of their shared dreams and aspirations.

With a steady hand, Nitin reached for Pallavi's nameplate, his heart heavy with the weight of his actions. As he affixed it to the door, he couldn't help but feel a pang of guilt for erasing Neel's presence from their shared workspace.

Next, Nitin turned his attention to the photographs adorning the walls, each frame a testament to the bond he had shared with Neel. With a sense of finality, he instructed his staff to remove their pictures and replace them with images of him and Pallavi.

As he held their photograph in his hands, Nitin's heart clenched with sorrow. The image captured a moment of joy and camaraderie, a snapshot of a time when their friendship knew no bounds. But now, it served as a painful reminder of what had been lost.

With a flick of his lighter, Nitin set the photograph ablaze, the flames licking at the edges as he watched Neel's face melt away into nothingness. But as the fire consumed the image, Nitin's mind played tricks on him, conjuring the illusion of Neel standing before him, his eyes filled with reproach.

"Nitin, what are you doing?" Neel's voice echoed in his mind, the sound reverberating through the empty office.

Nitin's hands trembled as he struggled to maintain his composure, his heart pounding in his chest. "I'm moving on, Neel. I have to," he whispered, his voice barely above a whisper.

But Neel's presence only seemed to grow stronger, his image flickering in and out of existence like a ghost haunting Nitin's every move. "You can't erase me from your life, Nitin. I'll always be a part of you," Neel's voice whispered in his ear, sending shivers down his spine.

Tears welled up in Nitin's eyes as he reached out to touch the apparition before him, his fingers passing through the empty air. "I miss you, Neel," he confessed, his voice choked with emotion.

But as quickly as he had appeared, Neel vanished, leaving Nitin alone in the darkness of his office. With a heavy heart, Nitin collapsed into his chair, the weight of his grief threatening to consume him.

In that moment of solitude, Nitin realized that no matter how hard he tried to move on, Neel would always be a part of him. And as he sat amidst the ashes of their shared memories, he knew that some bonds were too strong to be broken, even by the flames of change.

# NEEL

# Eclipsed Flames

The stage was bathed in a soft, ethereal glow as the curtains parted, revealing a world of beauty and tragedy meticulously crafted by Neel's creative vision. The audience held their collective breath, eager to immerse themselves in the emotional journey about to unfold before them.

As the music swelled, Vivian and Naveen stepped onto the stage, their movements fluid and graceful, a testament to the countless hours of rehearsal under Neel's meticulous direction. From the first gentle sway to the final, heart-wrenching embrace, they captivated the audience with the intensity of their performance.

But it was in the quiet moments, the pauses between each movement, that the true depth of their connection became apparent. As they locked eyes, a silent understanding passed between them, a shared understanding of the pain and longing that lay beneath the surface.

As the dance reached its climax, Neel's vision came to life in a crescendo of emotion and movement. Vivian and

Naveen moved as one, their bodies intertwined in a poignant display of love and loss. With each step, each gesture, they conveyed the tumultuous journey of two souls bound together by fate yet torn apart by circumstance.

In a haunting moment of clarity, Neel found himself lost in the illusion of his creation, his heart aching with the bittersweet realization of what could have been. As Vivian and Naveen danced as if their very lives depended on it, Neel saw himself and Nitin in their place, their movements echoing the passion and intensity of their once unbreakable bond.

But just as quickly as the illusion had come, it was shattered, torn apart by the harsh reality of their separation. As Vivian and Naveen were forced to part ways, the audience was left reeling, their hearts breaking for the star-crossed lovers whose love was destined to remain forever out of reach.

In that moment, Neel's masterpiece transcended the confines of the stage, touching the hearts of all who bore witness to its beauty. And as the final notes of the music faded into silence, there wasn't a dry eye in the house, for Neel had captured the essence of love and longing in a way that resonated with the deepest recesses of the soul.

.........

The university campus buzzed with excitement and jubilation as students and faculty reveled in the glory of their recent victory at the national dance competition. Neel, the mastermind behind the award-winning choreography, found himself at the center of attention, surrounded by a flurry of flashing cameras and eager reporters.

Despite the chaos around him, Neel remained composed, his demeanor radiating an air of quiet confidence. With every question thrown his way, he fielded them with grace and poise, his mind still basking in the euphoria of their triumph. Reporters lauded his innovative choreography, praising its intensity and emotional depth, and Neel couldn't help but feel a swell of pride at the recognition of his hard work.

"But Neel, your dance drama was not just about choreography; it was a journey of emotions. How did you manage to infuse such raw intensity into your performance?" another reporter inquired, her eyes alight with curiosity.

Neel's expression softened as he reflected on the creative process behind the dance drama. "For me, dance is a language of the soul," he replied thoughtfully. "I drew inspiration from my own experiences and emotions, channeling them into the movements to create a narrative that resonated with the audience."

The reporters nodded in understanding, captivated by Neel's insight into his artistic vision. But as the questions continued, delving into Neel's personal life and aspirations, he couldn't help but feel a twinge of discomfort. The spotlight, though flattering, also brought with it a sense of vulnerability, exposing the inner workings of his heart and mind to the scrutiny of the world.

"Neel, your work is deeply personal and evocative. Do you ever feel pressure to live up to the expectations of your audience?" another reporter pressed, her tone tinged with empathy.

Neel paused for a moment, his gaze distant as he considered the question. "Of course, there's always a certain level of pressure that comes with public recognition," he admitted. "But ultimately, my greatest motivation comes from within, from a desire to create art that speaks to the human experience and transcends cultural boundaries."

As the press conference drew to a close, Neel couldn't help but feel a sense of relief wash over him. The scrutiny of the media was both exhilarating and exhausting, a reminder of the delicate balance between fame and authenticity. Yet, amidst the whirlwind of attention, Neel remained grounded in his passion for dance, his unwavering dedication to his craft serving as a guiding light through the highs and lows of his journey.

Just then, Ridhima, , burst onto the scene with an air of urgency. "Bhaiya, we have to go back to India! It's Nitin bhai's wedding. Auntie called!" she exclaimed, her eyes sparkling with excitement.

As Neel and Ridhima discussed the prospect of returning to India for Nitin's wedding, Neel's phone buzzed with an incoming call. Glancing at the screen, he saw that it was Nitin's mother calling, her name flashing across the display.

With a mixture of anticipation and trepidation, Neel answered the call, his heart pounding in his chest. "Hello, aunty," he greeted, trying to keep his voice steady despite the whirlwind of emotions swirling within him.

"Neel beta, how are you?" Nitin's mother's voice was warm and familiar, a comforting presence even over the phone.

"I'm doing well, aunty. Thank you for asking," Neel replied, his mind racing with thoughts of Nitin's impending wedding and the possibility of their reunion.

"I'm calling to invite you and Ridhima to Nitin's wedding," Nitin's mother continued, her tone filled with genuine warmth and affection.

Neel's heart skipped a beat at the invitation, his emotions threatening to overwhelm him. "Thank you so much, aunty. We would be honored to attend," he responded, his voice tinged with gratitude.

As he hung up the phone, Neel felt a surge of emotions wash over him—gratitude for the invitation, hope for reconciliation, and a sense of longing for the friend he had lost. With Ridhima by his side and the prospect of Nitin's wedding looming on the horizon, Neel knew that their journey back to India would be filled with both joy and uncertainty, but he was determined to face whatever lay ahead with an open heart and a renewed sense of hope.

Ridhima's excitement was palpable as she grasped Neel's arm, her urgency evident in every word she spoke. "Bhaiya, it doesn't matter what happened in the past. Nitin bhai is getting married, and you have to be there to celebrate this new chapter in his life!" she insisted, her eyes shining with determination.

Neel's heart swelled with conflicting emotions as he listened to Ridhima's impassioned plea. "But Ridhima, what if my presence only serves to reopen old wounds? What if Nitin feels uncomfortable with me there?" he countered, his voice tinged with uncertainty.

Ridhima shook her head, her gaze unwavering as she met Neel's eyes. "Bhaiya, Nitin bhai may have his reservations, but deep down, he still cares about you. You can't let fear hold you back from being there for him on this important day," she urged, her words carrying the weight of conviction.

Neel's mind raced with doubt and hesitation, but the sincerity in Ridhima's words struck a chord within him. "You're right, Ridhima. I can't let my own fears dictate my actions. If Nitin bhai wants me there, then I'll be there for him, no matter what," he resolved, a sense of determination settling over him.

With Ridhima's unwavering support by his side, Neel knew that he could face whatever challenges lay ahead. As they made plans to return to India for Nitin's wedding, Neel couldn't help but feel a glimmer of hope stirring within him—a hope for reconciliation, and perhaps, a chance to mend the fractured bonds of their friendship.

The once vibrant atmosphere of the auditorium had transformed into a scene of chaos and despair, with thick smoke billowing out from the entrance and flames licking at the edges of the building. Neel's heart sank as he beheld the unfolding crisis, his mind racing with the urgency of the moment.

"Ridhima, I have to go!" Neel exclaimed, his voice resolute as he bolted towards the burning auditorium, leaving behind a bewildered group of reporters. His every step was fueled by determination, fueled by the thought of saving those trapped inside, including Vivan and Navin.

As he plunged into the heart of the inferno, memories of his estranged friend Nitin flooded Neel's mind. Despite the distance that had grown between them, Neel felt a tug of fate pulling them back together, perhaps for one final reckoning. With a sense of purpose guiding him, he braved the flames, ready to confront his past and fight for redemption.

Inside the blazing auditorium, Vivan and Navin found themselves trapped amidst the chaos. Determined to salvage their performance props, they remained behind as the flames raged around them. But when the structure began to collapse, they realized the gravity of their situation.

Amidst the blistering heat and falling debris, Neel dashed back into the burning building, refusing to leave his students behind. With his skin searing and his lungs filled with smoke, he guided Vivan and Navin through the inferno, inching towards safety with each perilous step.

But their path to freedom was obstructed by a sudden collapse, trapping them beneath a pile of rubble. Neel

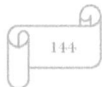

shielded his students from the falling debris, absorbing the brunt of the impact himself. Despite the agonizing pain coursing through his body, he refused to give up, determined to see Vivan and Navin to safety.

With Herculean effort, Neel managed to free them from the wreckage, but not without sustaining severe burns in the process. As they emerged from the burning auditorium, Neel collapsed, his body wracked with pain and exhaustion. Yet, his sacrifice had saved the lives of his students, and for that, he was hailed as a hero.

As they lay amidst the rubble, Vivan and Navin realized the magnitude of Neel's sacrifice. Despite their injuries, they were alive, thanks to his unwavering bravery and selflessness. And as they watched the flames consume the auditorium, they knew that they owed their lives to the man who had risked everything to save them.

As the ambulance doors closed behind him, Neel reached out and grasped the trembling hands of Navin and Vivan, his own voice quivering with emotion.

"Navin, Vivan," he began, his words carrying the weight of a lifetime's worth of mentorship and guidance, "I need you to remember something. No matter what lies ahead, never forget the lessons we've learned together. I may be leaving now, but I want you both to carry on, to embark on your new journeys with courage and resilience."

Navin's eyes glistened with unshed tears as he spoke, his voice choked with emotion. "But sir, you can't just leave us like this. We need you."

Neel's heart ached at Navin's words, but he knew that he had to reassure his students, even in the face of uncertainty. "I'll always be with you, in spirit if not in person. You have the strength to face whatever challenges come your way, I know it."

Vivan's voice trembled as he spoke, his gratitude overflowing. "Thank you, sir. For everything."

Neel smiled through his tears, his pride evident in his gaze. "You two have been my greatest students, my greatest achievements. Now, it's time for you to shine on your own."

As the ambulance pulled away, carrying Neel to safety, Navin and Vivan exchanged a meaningful glance. They knew that their mentor's sacrifice would forever shape their lives, guiding them as they ventured into an uncertain future. And as they faced the challenges ahead, they would draw strength from Neel's unwavering belief in their abilities, honoring his legacy with every step they took.

# Fragments of fate

In the hushed corridors of the hospital, where the relentless march of time seemed to slow to a standstill, Neel lay ensconced in the sterile embrace of the ICU. The rhythmic beeping of the monitors provided a somber backdrop to the silent vigil being kept by Nitin, who sat by Neel's bedside, grappling with the weight of unspoken truths and unresolved emotions that threatened to engulf them both.

"Nitin," Neel's voice was a fragile whisper in the dimly lit room, his gaze locked onto Nitin's with an intensity that mirrored the depths of his soul. "There's something I need to tell you."

Nitin's heart constricted at the vulnerability etched into every line of Neel's face, his resolve wavering in the face of Neel's silent plea. "What is it, Neel?" he replied, his voice barely above a whisper, laced with a mixture of trepidation and longing.

Neel's breath caught in his throat as he struggled to find the words to articulate the tangled mess of emotions swirling within him. "Nitin, I…" His voice faltered, his gaze dropping to his trembling hands as he grappled with the magnitude of what he was about to confess.

But Nitin reached out, his touch gentle yet unwavering, a silent reassurance of his unwavering support. "It's okay, Neel," he murmured, his voice a soothing balm against the backdrop of their shared turmoil. "You don't have to carry this burden alone."

Neel's eyes brimmed with unshed tears as he laid bare the depths of his soul, his words a poignant confession of his deepest desires and fears. "Nitin, I've spent so long trying to deny what I feel for you," he admitted, his voice thick with emotion. "But every time I close my eyes, all I see is you."

Nitin's heart ached with a bittersweet longing as he listened to Neel's heartfelt confession, his own emotions swirling in a tumultuous sea of regret and yearning. "Neel, you've always had a place in my heart," he confessed, his voice trembling with the weight of their shared history. "I've never stopped caring about you, not for a single moment."

As their conversation unfolded, the barriers that had long stood between them crumbled beneath the weight of their unspoken truths and unresolved emotions. "Nitin, that night," Neel began, his voice trembling with regret, "I realize now that it wasn't about physical pleasure for me. It was about something deeper, something more profound than I could ever put into words."

Nitin's heart constricted with a surge of compassion as he reached out to cup Neel's cheek, his touch igniting a spark of warmth within Neel's soul. "Neel, I understand," he murmured, his voice a gentle caress against the jagged edges of Neel's fractured heart. "And I forgive you."

As the echoes of their conversation lingered in the silence, Nitin felt a profound sense of peace wash over him, a quiet acceptance of the love he had long denied himself. And as he gazed into Neel's eyes, he knew that their bond was unbreakable, their connection eternal, bound together by threads of fate and the unspoken language of the heart.

As their spectral embrace faded into the ether, Neel was left alone in the darkness, his heart heavy with the weight of their shared history. And as the echoes of their conversation lingered in the silence, he knew that their bond transcended the boundaries of time and space, guiding them through the depths of their shared sorrow and into the light.

Meanwhile, in the hospital room, Vivan and Naveen stood vigil by Neel's bedside, their hearts heavy with worry and uncertainty. Each beep of the heart monitor served as a stark reminder of the fragility of life and the preciousness of their mentor's presence.

"He's going to make it through this, Vivan," Naveen declared, his voice filled with quiet resolve. "We won't let him slip away, not after everything we've been through together."

With renewed determination, Vivan nodded in agreement, his eyes shining with unshed tears. "We'll be here for him, every step of the way," he vowed, his voice filled with unwavering conviction. "Because that's what family does."

# NITIN

# Eternal Embrace

The famous beach resort in Goa shimmered under the soft glow of twinkling lights, its beauty accentuated by the presence of industry insiders and who's who of the town. It was a momentous occasion, marked by the wedding of Nitin, the renowned choreographer. As the time drew near, Nitin stood in the mandap, adorned in a golden sherwani and a pink turban, his heart pounding with anticipation.

Surrounded by bustling activity, Nitin's mind was consumed by a whirlwind of emotions. Despite the joyous atmosphere, a sense of unease gnawed at his heart. He knew that the time had come to move forward, to leave behind the shadow of Neel and embrace the promise of a new beginning. But the thought of forgetting Neel, of erasing his memory from his life, weighed heavily on Nitin's conscience. He couldn't shake the feeling that he was betraying his friend, abandoning him.

As Nitin scanned the crowd, his restless gaze searching for any sign of Neel, he couldn't help but feel a pang of disappointment each time his search proved futile. Pallavi had informed him that Ridhima had been invited by their mother, adding to Nitin's anticipation and anxiety. With each passing moment, the anticipation of Neel's arrival grew, but there was no sign of him.

Despite his best efforts to push aside his lingering doubts and fears, Nitin found himself unable to shake the feeling of unease that gripped his heart. The weight of his decision loomed heavy on his shoulders, casting a shadow over what should have been a joyous occasion. And as he stood in the midst of celebration, surrounded by loved ones and well-wishers, Nitin couldn't help but wonder if he was making the right choice.

The decor of the venue, resplendent with vibrant colors and intricate designs, served as a stark contrast to Nitin's tumultuous thoughts. Each detail, meticulously crafted to perfection, seemed to mock Nitin's inner turmoil, a reminder of the beauty that surrounded him even in the midst of chaos. And as the ceremony began, Nitin found himself lost in a sea of emotions, torn between the past and the promise of the future.

As the wedding rituals unfolded, Nitin's heart was heavy with regret and longing. He knew that he couldn't undo the past, couldn't change the choices he had made. But as he exchanged vows with Pallavi, promising to love and cherish her for eternity, Nitin made a silent vow to himself. He would honor Neel's memory, keep him alive in his heart, and never forget the bond they shared. For even in the midst of celebration, Neel's absence was a constant reminder of the price of love and the burden of regret.

As Pallavi stumbled, Nitin's heart clenched with panic, his mind racing as he lunged forward to prevent her fall. In that split second, his thoughts were consumed by Neel, his eternal companion who seemed to haunt his every waking moment. "Neel, hold yourself together," he murmured under his breath, a desperate plea to a ghost from his past. "I won't let you leave me behind."

As he extended his hand to grasp Neel's imaginary presence, a jolt of realization coursed through him. He had been holding Pallavi all along, her form now tangible in his arms. Confusion and guilt washed over him as he struggled to reconcile the conflicting emotions swirling within him.

"Pallavi," Nitin whispered, his voice barely above a whisper as he met her gaze, his eyes filled with a mixture of gratitude and anguish. "I'm sorry. I didn't mean to—"

But Pallavi cut him off, her own voice trembling with emotion as she implored him to confront the truth that lay buried within his heart. "Nitin, you must understand," she pleaded, her words carrying the weight of undeniable truth. "During the rituals, you were with Neel, not me. How long will you deceive yourself about your love?"

Nitin's heart constricted at her words, a painful reminder of the love he had long denied himself. "Love transcends the physical," Pallavi continued, her voice soft but resolute. "Don't degrade it in this manner. You and Neel are one soul; how will you divide this life?"

In that moment, Nitin felt the walls he had built around his heart begin to crumble, the weight of years of denial and self-deception bearing down upon him. As he gazed into Pallavi's eyes, he knew that he could no longer hide from the truth that lay buried within his soul. It was time to confront his feelings for Neel, to embrace the love that had always been his guiding light in the darkness. And with Pallavi's unwavering support by his side, he knew that he could finally begin to unravel the tangled web of emotions that bound him to Neel, his eternal companion, his soulmate.

Nitin felt the weight of Pallavi's words like a heavy burden on his chest, crushing him with their undeniable truth. She had seen through his facade, stripping away the layers of denial and exposing the raw vulnerability of his heart. As he struggled to process her revelation, Nitin found himself grappling with a tumult of emotions, each one vying for dominance within his conflicted soul.

Pallavi's words reverberated in his mind, a haunting echo that stirred a whirlwind of memories and emotions. Images of Neel flashed before his eyes, each one a painful reminder of the bond they shared, a connection that transcended the boundaries of friendship. Try as he might, Nitin could no longer deny the depth of his feelings for Neel; they were an intrinsic part of him, woven into the very fabric of his being.

As the scene unfolded around him in slow motion, Nitin stood frozen in place, torn between duty and desire. The realization dawned upon him with stunning clarity, illuminating the path forward with an irrefutable certainty. And as he met Pallavi's gaze, he knew that he could no longer hide from the truth that lay within his heart.

In that moment of revelation, Nitin felt a profound sense of clarity wash over him, cleansing him of the doubts and insecurities that had plagued him for so long. He understood, with unwavering certainty, that his life could only be complete with Neel by his side. As he looked into Neel's eyes, he saw not just his past, but his present and future entwined with his love, and he knew that there was no turning back.

Yet, amidst the whirlwind of emotions that threatened to overwhelm him, Nitin felt a pang of guilt towards Pallavi. He wanted to apologize, to explain, but before he could find the words, Pallavi took matters into her own hands. With a quiet determination, she reached into her bag, retrieved an envelope, and placed it gently in Nitin's hand.

"Nitin, this is your ticket to London," Pallavi said softly, her voice tinged with both understanding and compassion. "I was certain that this sacred fire would guide you towards the right path. Go, reclaim your life."

Nitin stared down at the envelope, feeling the weight of Pallavi's gesture settle upon his shoulders like a mantle of grace. Despite the ache in his heart, he felt a surge of gratitude towards Pallavi for her unwavering support and understanding. With a heavy but determined heart, he nodded, silently acknowledging the significance of her gesture. And as he prepared to embark on his journey, he knew that he carried Pallavi's blessings with him, guiding him towards a future filled with love, redemption, and the promise of a new beginning.

# The Unyielding Bond

As Nitin stood amidst the bustling chaos of London Airport, the world around him seemed to blur into a whirlwind of noise and movement. His heart raced erratically in his chest, each beat echoing with the weight of impending dread. Then, like a sudden bolt of lightning, the news headline flashed across the screen before him, igniting a firestorm of emotions within his soul.

"Buckinghamshire New University's Dance Department Head and renowned Indian dance director, Neil, showing signs of recovery," the headline blared, each word a dagger plunging into Nitin's already fragile heart. Time seemed to freeze around him as he grappled with the magnitude of the news. Neil, his mentor, his confidant, was fighting for his life, and Nitin was miles away, powerless to do anything but watch.

A montage of memories flickered through Nitin's mind, each one a testament to the bond they shared – the countless hours spent in rehearsal, the whispered dreams of success, the unspoken understanding that bound them together. Tears stung at the corners of his eyes as he struggled to comprehend the gravity of the situation. Neil was more than just a mentor; he was family, a guiding light in Nitin's darkest hours.

Despite the urgency of the situation, Nitin found himself rooted to the spot, his legs heavy with the weight of indecision. Every fiber of his being screamed for him to move, to rush to Neil's side and offer whatever solace he could. But fear held him captive, a suffocating grip that threatened to consume him whole.

As the images on the screen shifted to show Neil lying motionless in a hospital bed, surrounded by a labyrinth of machines and tubes, Nitin felt a surge of anguish tear through him. The sight was a stark reminder of Neil's mortality, a brutal awakening to the fragility of life itself. Questions swirled in his mind like a tempestuous storm – How had this happened? What could he do to help? – but answers remained elusive, slipping through his fingers like grains of sand.

With a trembling hand, Nitin reached for his luggage, his heart heavy with a sense of impending doom. Every fiber of his being screamed for him to act, to do something, anything, to ease Neil's suffering. And as he took his first tentative steps forward, a silent prayer echoed in his soul, a desperate plea for Neil's recovery, for a miracle to light the way through the darkness that threatened to consume them both.

Amidst the cacophony of chaos swirling within his mind, a voice pierced through the turmoil – a voice that resonated with familiarity and longing, as if reaching out from a distant memory. It was Neil, calling out to him, his words carrying across the vast expanse that separated them like a lifeline in the darkness.

"No, Neil, you'll pull through. Your Nitin is here," Nitin murmured, his voice trembling with raw emotion. His hand instinctively sought the tattoo etched upon his wrist – a symbol of their shared bond, an unspoken promise of eternal connection.

With a surge of determination coursing through his veins, Nitin seized his luggage and charged towards the exit, his heart pounding with a singular purpose – to stand by Neil's side, to offer him the solace and support he so desperately craved. Each step forward was a testament to their unwavering friendship, a pledge to weather the storm together, no matter the cost.

As he stepped into the waiting taxi, the weight of the moment bore down upon him, threatening to engulf him in a tidal wave of emotions. Tears welled in his eyes, a testament to the depth of his love for Neil, for the bond they shared that transcended time and distance.

Through tear-streaked eyes, Nitin gazed out at the sprawling cityscape, his heart heavy with the weight of uncertainty yet buoyed by a glimmer of hope. For Neil, for their friendship, for the unbreakable bond that tethered them together, he would brave any storm, scale any obstacle, and defy the odds to ensure that their connection endured, unyielding and eternal.

# forever fades Away

In the hospital room, the chaos of Neel's deteriorating condition filled the air like a suffocating fog, punctuated by the frantic efforts of the medical staff to save him. The steady beep of machines provided a dissonant backdrop to the urgency that hung heavy in the room, each blip of the monitor a grim reminder of Neel's fading vitality.

As Neel's heartbeat grew fainter, the nurses' urgent calls for assistance echoed through the halls, a desperate plea for a miracle to halt the relentless march of fate. But despite the doctors' tireless efforts, Neel's condition continued to worsen, his body succumbing to the relentless assault of illness.

In the midst of it all, Riddhima stood by helplessly, her heart breaking with each passing moment. Her eyes brimmed with unshed tears as she watched the man she loved slip further and further away, a helpless witness to the cruel whims of destiny.

Neel's gaze wandered towards the door, a glimmer of recognition flickering in his eyes amidst the haze of pain and exhaustion. "Nitin," he murmured weakly, his voice barely audible amidst the chaos that enveloped him. But Nitin was nowhere to be seen, his absence a painful absence that added to Neil's growing sense of isolation.

As Neil's breaths grew shallower, his hand trembled, reaching out for something – anything – to hold onto. It found only emptiness, a stark reminder of the absence of the one person who had always been by his side. Memories flooded his mind, flashes of laughter and shared moments that now felt like distant echoes of a life once lived.

With a final, labored breath, Neil's hand fell limply to the side, his eyes fluttering shut as he succumbed to the inevitable. The room fell silent, save for the soft hum of medical equipment, as the doctors bowed their heads in solemn resignation, their efforts to save him ultimately in vain.

But even as Neel's physical presence faded from the world, his spirit lingered on in the hearts of those who loved him. And in that final moment of peace, amidst the quiet stillness of the hospital room, Neel found solace in the memories of his bond with Nitin, their shared laughter and moments of intimacy echoing in his mind as he slipped away into eternity.

As Neel slipped away into the embrace of eternity, the world seemed to come to a standstill, a hushed reverence settling over the hospital room. His departure left behind a palpable emptiness, a void that echoed with the memories of a life once lived and a love that knew no bounds.

Just as the last vestiges of life faded from Neel's form, the door creaked open, and Nitin entered the room. His heart clenched with anguish as he beheld the scene before him – the stillness of Neel's body, the solemn faces of the medical staff.

With tear-filled eyes, Nitin approached Neel's bedside, his footsteps echoing in the silence that enveloped the room. He reached out tentatively, his trembling hand hovering over Neel's cold, lifeless form, a silent farewell to the love they had shared.

Beside Neil's bed stood the breakfast trolley, adorned with a single plate bearing a red rose and a note – a tradition Neil had always upheld, a symbol of their enduring love. As Nitin read the note, his breath caught in his throat, his heart breaking anew with each word that spoke of love and longing.

"Welcome back, Nitin," the note whispered, a bittersweet reminder of the life they had planned together, now shattered beyond repair. Tears welled in Nitin's eyes, blurring the inked words that promised a future that would never come to pass.

In that moment, amidst the overwhelming grief, Nitin felt the weight of their shared dreams and aspirations, the unspoken promises that now lay shattered at his feet. His heart ached with the unbearable pain of loss, a gaping hole left in its wake by Neel's untimely departure.

As Nitin bowed his head in silent mourning, he knew that their love would live on, a beacon of light in the darkness that threatened to consume him. In Neel's final

gesture – his outstretched hand reaching for an empty plate, as if welcoming Nitin into the void – Nitin found solace in the knowledge that they would be together again, if only in spirit.

With a heavy heart and tear-stained cheeks, Nitin bid farewell to the love of his life, his soul forever haunted by the memory of a love lost too soon. And as he left the room, his footsteps echoing in the empty corridors, the world seemed a little darker, a little emptier, without Neel by his side. But in the depths of his despair, Nitin found a flicker of hope – a belief that their love would endure, transcending the boundaries of time and space, until they were reunited once more.

And

Forever fades away

www.ingramcontent.com/pod-product-compliance
Lightning Source LLC
LaVergne TN
LVHW041946070526
838199LV00051BA/2918